Keridan's Journey

Siren Elementals Book One

Michelle Peterson

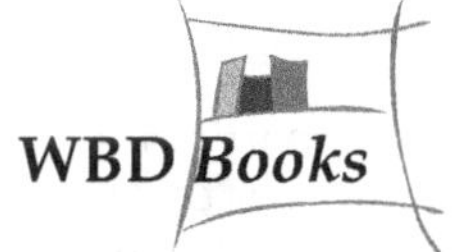

Keridan's Journey

This book is a work of fiction. Names, characters, incidents and places are used fictitiously and any resemblance to actual people living or non-living, actual events or places are entirely coincidental.

Inquiries should be addressed to
WBDBooks
PO Box 51
Duluth, GA 30096 USA
www.wbdbooks.com

FIRST EDITION

First Printing (February 2011)

Catalog Data
Peterson, Michelle
Keridan's Journey
Library of Congress Control Number: 2010943276
ISBN 9780983045106 Pbk

Cover illustration by: Michelle W Peterson

Printed in the United States of America

ACKNOWLEDGEMENTS

To those who listened endlessly, I thank you.

To those who supported relentlessly, I thank you.

CONTENTS

Prologue – Thirty Years Ago....7
Chapter 1 - My Mother Kept Secrets....11
Chapter 2 – I Met My Father Over Ice Cream....19
Chapter 3 – I Become A Superhero....29
Chapter 4 – Crazy People And Downward Dog....35
Chapter 5 – I Mourn For Opportunities Lost....45
Chapter 6 – Royal Bloodlines....51
Chapter 7 – Coffee and Competition....61
Chapter 8 – Friends Don't Let Friends Bowl Mad....69
Chapter 9 – I See Kidnapped People....77
Chapter 10 – I Played At The Park....85
Chapter 11 - Party Crasher....93
Chapter 12 – What Are You?....103
Chapter 13 – I Lose My Temper…Again....117
Chapter 14 – Where For Art Thou, Robert?....131
Chapter 15 – Plane Rides Make Me Nervous....139
Chapter 16 - New Places, New Faces....147
Chapter 17 – Bedtime Stories....157
Chapter 18 – The Depth Of Love....165
Chapter 19 – I Met Myself....179
Chapter 20 – I Date A Deity....193
Chapter 21 – Sweet Torture....205
Chapter 22 - Ultimatums....217
Chapter 23 – Hallucinations And Epiphanies....229
Chapter 24 – Missing Pieces....237
Chapter 25 – Bumps And Bruises....243
Chapter 26 – Is This The End?....253

Prologue – Thirty Years Ago

The archaeologists gently brushed away centuries of earth hoping to reveal more details of the carved stone that lay beneath them. This place was sacred to not only the small cadre of students that discovered it but also to the local tribes that gathered everyday to witness the progress.

On the tenth day of the dig, something strange occurred. One of the students, Bhalil Kanari, uncovered some primitive writings that on first glance appeared much older than the rest of the site. While he was documenting the find he went into a trance like state of mind and his body fell to the ground.

His fellow students grew alarmed and Bhalil

was rushed to the local hospital. The entire time he continued to mumble incoherently.

While the dig team was distracted by their fallen team member, two seemingly simple local men approached the place where Bhalil had lain.

In a voice just above a whisper, the first man spoke, "This is not the right time for them to gain knowledge. This generation lacks the faith and conviction to handle absolute truths."

"You may be right. The key however has already unlocked a portion of the history. You know as well as I what it takes to stop the cycle once it has begun."

"The old ways have died out. No one alive will even understand how to decipher the signs. We may still have some time."

"There are still a few who cling to the old ways. I feel the energy. I also feel a disturbance that has been brewing for some time with our neighbors. Their problems will soon be ours I fear."

"What of the prophecy?"

"I do not feel that energy yet. We must remain patient. There will be one who saves our existence."

Both men looked down at the primitive writings

on the carved stone beneath their feet. "We must still take precautions against those who might abuse the knowledge." With that a red light shot from their hands and blasted the stone carvings until the markings were eroded beyond any recollection.

"What of the boy?"

"His mind will right itself but his life will be doomed to tragedy. It is the way of all Seerers."

The two men passed unnoticed through the throng of student workers. When they reached the rock-strewn base that ran around the site they disappeared between the cracks of the rock.

Chapter 1 – My Mother kept Secrets

I saw things in my head – things that would happen, could happen. I always had an uncanny knack for knowing why someone should not do something. My mother called it a gift but it was never something we advertised. I did not want to be locked up in a crazy house.

I could only get flashes from people I knew and even then the flashes only came when they wanted to. Trust me. I used to try to get some insight on my calculus exams in college but not even a hint would flash into my mind.

After waking up for the second time, I went about my daily routine. I slept fine however I still felt unnerved for some reason. It was spring time in Atlanta, Georgia and with the exception of the high pollen count and haze, I loved springtime here. Cherry blossoms and dogwoods were abundant enough to never need perfume. All you had to do was stand outside for a few minutes and you would instantly be infused with a wonderfully natural floral smell. Today would be a good ditch day.

My daydreams were interrupted by the shrill sound of my phone echoing through the house. I knew something bad was about to happen. The ring was different. Pictures flew into my head of my mom lying in a bed. I answered the phone and listened numbly. Somehow I grabbed my keys and ran to the door. My emotions led to some really erratic driving down Interstate 85. Luckily, no cops were out today. I arrived at the hospital frantic. I never had been able to handle bad news well.

Doctors and nurses hovered over my mother. Her coppery skin was pallid and translucent. The normally small grey streaks in her black hair had seemingly taken over her entire head. Her topaz eyes locked on mine and she whispered, "Keridan." I leaned closer. "Keridan, I need some time. Just ask them for a few minutes for me." I turned to the closest doctor but was stopped by her hand. "Not them...just ask." Something in her eyes made my stomach ball. Pictures flew in my head and I saw these beautiful creatures flying in front of me. I reached out to them and begged for just a few more minutes for my mom.

A lot of things happened at once. I immediately was in a forest grove with flowers around me and my mother was resting in a hammock nearby. She looked up, saw me and rushed over. "Keridan, thank you so much for asking; tell your father I said I am in debt to him again."

Having been a test tube baby, I felt this was a strange request. I knew I was dreaming. The smells, the colors are only this vibrant in a dream. My mother was lying on a bed in a hospital gown not prancing about in a fairy dress.

"Keridan, I do not know how much time I have so let me start. There are things I never told you. There are worlds I never dared reveal. Your father was a Man Siren. You are half Siren."

"Mom, you know my father was Number 5148691. What are you talking about?"

"Yes, that part was true but the man behind the number was a Siren. You are very special. Years ago when I found out I was told to keep it from you so you could be safe but you need to know now. Keridan, I am dying. Somehow my presence has masked you from the others but it will not be for much longer. As soon as I am gone, things will start to happen to you."

"Mom, whoa...what are you talking about? I do not understand. What's a Siren? What's going to happen to me? You can't die. I need you. I need you to *not* give up!"

"Keridan, baby, listen carefully. Sirens are these enchanted beings. There are like healers of the mind and soul." The scene flicked between the forest and the hospital. "I am running out of time. You have the ability to see things sweetheart. Those flashes you always are getting, that is your gift. People are drawn to you but it will become so much more intense. Be wary of this. Trust only your heart." The scene flicked again. I had a thousand questions. I did not know where the dream stopped and reality began.

I blinked and my mom's eyes briefly looked afraid. "Trust your pictures. Trust your heart. Trust your father." With that, the woman I had loved for twenty-five years was gone. Her lifeless eyes bore a gaping hole in my heart.

Doctors stilled around me and everyone seemed to be moving in slow motion. Nurses patted my shoulders. Tears fell from my eyes. My breath became short. I started walking backwards. The room was spinning and then there was nothing. No sounds. No air.

I knew I had passed out when I could feel the ice packs on my forehead. One of the nurses leaned over me. "It's okay sweetie. You just fainted. Lie still for a while."

The doctor came in. "Ms. Patrick, I am so sorry for your loss."

"Please call me Keridan. Ms. Patrick was my mother."

"Are you able to talk for a few minutes?"

"Sure."

"I have some forms for you to sign. Your mom asked for me to give you these when the time came."

"What do you mean?"

He shifted nervously and ran his fingers through his hair. "Keridan, somehow your mother knew she was dying. We didn't find anything wrong with her physically. She insisted on filling out all the paperwork and making the necessary preparations. She had me call you when she was at a stopping point." He paused to look at me. His eyes burned with an intensity not often directed at me. "If there is anything I can do for you, don't hesitate to call." He didn't look as if he was talking about my mother anymore.

I tried to make some distance between me and the good doctor. "Uh, thanks Doctor."

I needed some air. I filled out the paper work and headed home. I stopped to pick up some Chinese food. The man behind the counter professed his undying love to me out of the blue. I bumped the waiter and he broke out into song. The homeless man on the street started to follow me.

I got in my car and drove up Interstate 85 North as fast as I could. This was just too much to process in one day. I needed to cry. I deserved my release. My mom...my best friend left me today. The magnitude of that fact had not sunk in yet. I made it back to the house and crawled into my favorite chair and let it all out.

After literally hours, I sat down and ate my now cold food. I picked up the folder from my mom. There was a letter.

Dear Keridan,

Don't be sad baby. I know this seems sudden but I am prepared. I don't know if I will get a chance to explain everything to you so I need you to open our mind a bit. There is a world outside Atlanta and you are about to go for an adventure.

Your father's name is Alexo. Now that I am gone he will be able to contact you. Listen to his story, sweetheart. I can't say anymore.

I have tried to make this as easy for you as I can. I know that is saying a lot but you were the best thing that ever happened to me. I would not have changed a thing.

Be prepared to experience life that is beyond science. When you think that there is no explanation for things understand that sometimes an explanation is not needed. You are beautiful and strong. Allow yourself to love and be loved in returned.

For Ever Yours,

Mom

Chapter 2 – I Met My Father Over Ice Cream

My mom truly had taken care of everything. She had already arranged with the funeral home for her cremation. Her house was packed up. She had marked what was to come to me and go to others. She even arranged for the movers to contact me to pick everything up. She had the insurance on standby waiting to send me a check.

It was like she wanted me to just go on about my day with as little stress as I could. It was surreal. She kept this a secret from me for all these years. No one could be this prepared unless they had known for a long time. She prepared for everything except the emptiness in my heart.

The week after my mom died I did not go out much. I lounged on the couch and ate a lot of black walnut ice cream. I had never felt like an adult until this moment. Reality began to set in. Her death began to set in. I kept picking up the phone to call her. I was just surviving on ice cream with no appetite for anything else. At some point I would need to actually buy some more food which would necessitate the need to go back to work. I had to put one foot in front of the other and just move forward.

On day eight of my new adulthood, there came a knock on my door. There stood the most beautiful man I had ever seen. He was dark skinned with clear light brown eyes. In fact, they were the same shade as mine. His smile was soft and it framed his perfectly white teeth. He stood there with two cups of coffee and a carton of ice cream.

"Keridan, I am glad to finally meet you." He waited expectantly for some response from me. Pictures flew into my head of him...flashes from different times of my life.

"You're my father!" That sounded strange coming from my mouth but somehow I knew that he had to be. I always expected to have some sort of emotional reaction to finally seeing my father but I had never envisioned meeting like this. I was having an out of body experience. I could not hate this man. It was not like he abandoned me or my mother. I have known for twenty-five years that I did not have a father. I came to accept that but seeing this man with my eyes look at me with such kindness made me explode. He was somehow a living connection to my mother.

"Yes, Keridan…May I come in?" I showed him in and he handed me a cup of my favorite coffee. "Drink, dear. I know you must have a thousand questions so where would you like to start?"

There was a calmness that washed over me. It felt like a blanket was wrapped around my shoulders and someone was hugging me. I looked at this man who was waiting patiently for me to start hammering him with questions. He seemed ageless. I no longer believed in fairy tales but he was definitely the prince charming type.

"How are you my father? If you have known about me why did you wait twenty-five years to show up?"

He chuckled to himself. "Well, let's see. First,

my name is Alexo. I have known about you since before you were born. How much do you know about mythical beings?" I shook my head. "Well, then let me go back a bit. Your mom told you that I was a Siren. In my world, Sirens have become endangered. So we have had to become creative to ensure our existence. Your mother was chosen to bear a child for us."

He paused, waited for me to catch up. "After you were born your mother was given twenty-five years on her life until your abilities would no longer be dormant. I have watched over you but I was not allowed to contact you until after your protector has transitioned."

"What's transitioned?"

"Before you were born we contacted your mom to explain things to her. She went into her pregnancy with the knowledge that she may not live through it. You see Sirens are born fully grown. We were not sure what would happen. She kept saying that she would be alright. You kept sending her flashes of your life together." He paused. "We thought everything would be okay...but it became difficult. You were very intense, more so than we could ever have planned for. We were going to lose you. We had enough energy to repair one soul. Your mother begged for your life but we knew you could not exist without her...your protector. So we split the energy to give her some. She had enough life force to see you through until now. Her spirit has transitioned beyond the realms of our land."

I was gripping the table at this point. My mind was spinning. As strange as this story sounded I believed at least some portions of it. Tears fell freely down my face and the wound in my heart began to fester. He reached out and touched my elbow. "You fell from the swing when you were five and had to get stitches here." As he rubbed my elbow, the twenty year old scar vanished.

Being super emotional and equally neurotic, I dropped my coffee immediately. I stood up and stumbled backwards until I hit the wall. "Whoa! First you tell me that I am some sort of freakish hybrid experiment. Then you go on to say that I am basically the reason my mom is dead right now. Now you work some voodoo magic on my arm. Mister, I don't know what game you are playing at but I am so not the one."

"I am Keridan Patrick. I will give you the fact that we may be related. I have your features but you must have spent a night at Bellevue before coming here." I started looking around my house for hidden cameras.

Alexo laughed. It was filled with curiosity and disappointment. "Keridan, I know this is a lot to process. Do I understand correctly that you believe that I am your father?"

That somehow I could believe. I had his eyes, his nose and we shared the same misplaced dimple. True, this was not as conclusive as a DNA test but I was willing to concede. "Yes, I think you are the same man my mom spoke of."

"Good. Do you believe that I am not altogether human?"

That is where we hit a snag. "I have come to grips with the fact that I live in my own little world but even that world doesn't have fairies, pixies or Sirens."

He seemed to reflect carefully. "What would it take to convince you that I am what I say I am?" At that point his eyes changed from a brilliant topaz to what look like pure white light. He started to rise out of his seat and sort of float. His ears became pointy and his face glowed. He had an aura surrounding him. I recognized that he was one of the angels I thought I saw in the hospital. "What would it take, Keridan?" He hovered close to me and grabbed my hand. Pulling me up in the air, he spun me around as if we were dancing a dance. He put me down and then placed his hand over my heart. I instantly saw pictures in my head of my whole childhood. I could see him there always hovering around me. He was like a little sprite sitting on my shoulder directing me. I saw flashes of his world and the beauty of it.

I blinked and he was back to normal walking casually backing to his cup of coffee. "What am I then? I saw in your head. I felt love emanating from your memories. I am left with a strange sensation...an overload of emotion. I don't know how else to explain it."

"To answer your question – you are part Siren. You are the first ever hybrid. You comprise the best parts of the two species. Sirens are fabled for their beauty and mind manipulating abilities. We are not affected by time per se. We can project thoughts and images into the minds of others to help control emotions. We use this as a protection mechanism as well as for our peace keeping efforts."

"What do you mean *peace keeping*? Are you like

the United Nations for enchanted creatures?"

"No, our world is connected to this world; but just as the sun makes things grows here, emotions control my world. Specifically, the emotion of this world is our energy. I should say this dimension. There is a small sect of Sirens that are in charge of keeping the balance in place in order to sustain our life. You could call us the equivalent of your FBI. We each have certain gifts. Every Siren's gift is slightly different. For example, you have the gift of *Insight* - the ability to see paths or glimpses of people's future or past. I have observed that your pictures, as you like to call them, are a bit sporadic. You also have now inherited the Siren's call."

"What's the Siren's call?"

"The Siren's call is what makes others drawn to you. It seems particularly strong in you. I think it has a lot to do with your human side. You are a very attractive human. If you add that to my DNA there is no man that would be able to resist you. That could be a problem though." He said the last part with a little twinkle in his eye. "We like to keep a low profile in this realm. It is essential to keep our world a secret. I will get your aunts to help teach you how to control it. I will help you develop your other skills. He seems to finally notice my mouth drop. "Which part did I loose you on the beautiful, the aunts, or your new mystical powers?" He chuckled.

"All of it really, but I think I am shocked I have aunts. It has always been just me and mom. Now it seems from her death I inherited a family. It's weird." I shook off my awe. "How long are you here for?" That came off sounding strange but I just noticed a stack of papers that I had been putting off going through. It seemed like the real world was creeping slowly back into the fantasy land.

"I am here for as long as you need me. I have to prepare you. The protections your mother had in place are wearing off. Soon you will be visible to others. Don't worry we have been preparing for this. I think I have overwhelmed you enough for one day."

"Can you stay here with me so I won't wake up and think I dreamed it all?"

"I have been here with you."

"Ok, then...let me clarify. Can you stay here where I can see you? You know less Siren – more human."

"Well sure if that helps. Keridan, please understand that you are most precious to me. You are my only child and as strange as it may seem to you right now, I am very protective of you."

I blushed in spite of myself. I think I could get used to being protected. I walked right past my stack of papers and went to sleep.

Chapter 3 – I Become A Superhero

Over the next week I eased back into work. I was a freelance project manager and an artist. My mother had insisted that I focus on doing something creative and something in the business world. She thought it would round me out. It gave me a wide berth of flexibility with my time as well as focused me on meeting deadlines. During the day I worked on my projects from home. I had an art show coming up and I needed to finish some paintings. During the evening, "the aunties", as they like to be called tried to teach me how to control my abilities. I became amazed at how much super natural things I could not only accept but also believe. I looked differently at the world now. I did not just live in the suburbs of Atlanta, Georgia. There was actually a hidden world literally right *inside* my door.

Alexo and his sisters could shimmer which meant they could disappear altogether. That was how they traveled. I was disappointed to find out that I was not able to do that. I doubted that I could maintain the mental acuity to handle all these new sensations.

Alexo drilled me until my mind was numb. He was trying to test the limitations of my powers. "Let's try this again."

"I don't think I can go again." I rubbed my temples. "Why do I need to? What's the rush?"

"You have a very important job to do and you need to be prepared." He said flatly. "Look at it like this...You are a project manager for an art firm. Let's just imagine for a moment that three of your critical team members just quit the project. You still have deadlines but now there are not enough people to finish on time. Every moment added to your schedule cost money in penalties and fines. At stake is your reputation, your job and your financial security. These are definite motivators to get the job done as quickly as possible. If you apply the same scenario to the Sirens then you can empathize with our cause. We are peace keepers. For millennia after millennia we have aided the human race in maintaining some semblance of non aggression. No focus is drawn on ourselves. We are the whispers in people's minds. Someone is trying to upset our project but instead of loss of job security it would mean world chaos in both your realm and mine. Sirens are disappearing weekly. We are stretched thin. Someone knows of us and is exploiting it. You, Keridan, are our secret weapon. That is why I am pushing you so hard. We do not know who is behind the attacks. I can not take any precautions with you." He looked at me so fiercely I felt my hands shaking.

I looked around my front room trying to break the hold he had over me. "I think you are putting too much stock in my abilities. I can't leap over a building or fly. I can't project thoughts like you. If there is some big bad out there I wouldn't be able to help. I am not trying be a pessimist but let's be real about it."

"That's not entirely true, dear. You have some unique abilities. You can receive different outcomes of future happenings although you can only see the paths themselves and not what is ultimately chosen."

"Yes, but it changes with every decision a person makes. I don't have to see the person but I do have to have some emotional connection to that person. That has to be a major limitation. I also have never seen any future paths that involved me."

"I think with practice your flashes will develop more." He patted my shoulders.

The flashes were actually a cool super power to have until they became so overwhelming that it gave me headaches. In fact it was so mentally draining that when I did fall asleep at night, I did not even dream.

Alexo found that my emotions triggered or hindered my new found gifts. I could keep my Siren's call at bay as long as I was not extremely distracted. If I became angry, overjoyed or even depressed my call would go into overdrive. It seems to affect men, women and even animals. Although, I could not project thoughts into peoples head I could project emotions but even they were limited to emotions like sadness or mental despair – nothing that was associated to anything physical.

"So, back to the bad guy…How am I to help?"

"Well, somehow your human side has affected your Siren side. It seems your abilities are the opposite of a pure Siren. We project thoughts while you can receive thoughts – well your pictures. I think with time and practice more of your abilities will surface. This works in our favor. Whatever is affecting the Sirens wouldn't work the same on you. From what we can gather, the missing Sirens can't communicate with us which leads us to believe that someone or something is targeting our specific abilities. If we can mask your Siren side until we know more then we are in a better position to tamper down World War 12."

"What happens if you can't mask my Siren side?"

His perfect face showed just a trace of fear for a moment. "I won't sugar coat anything for you. You would be in grave danger. If you are important to my kind just imagine how important you would be to others." He laughed a little and put his arm around my shoulders. "Always remember that I love you and will do anything in my power to not let anything happen to you."

I truly understood that I had to get my emotions in check before I ventured away from my protective bubble.

Chapter 4 – Crazy People And Downward Dog

I was painting more and that was helping me clear my head. My paintings however started to reflect the pictures that flew into my head. Old boyfriends, my favorite grocery store lady and even one of my neighbors were regular features in my watercolors.

Alexo suggested that I take up yoga to help with my headaches and concentration. I was on my way to the studio for my first class when he shimmered into my car. I still had not gotten use to that and almost ran off the road.

"Dude, can you give me some warning next time. Help this poor human out!"

He looked up at me and smiled. "What fun would that be?" He waved off my retort before it could get out of my mouth. "Something has come up. I am going to have to leave you for a little while." My heart began to sink and little waves of despair started to creep over me. Amazingly, these past few weeks were enough for a deep connection to grow between Alexo and me. "The aunties will be with you to watch over you. Don't look so miserable."

"But we were just getting to know each other. We had a routine. What has happened?"

"Do you remember when I told you we were disappearing? Well, one of my informants has a lead. I need to go check it out. You need to stay here and practice your gifts. Soon you will have to fight off more than just men." He patted my hand. "I know the past few weeks in no way compensate for twenty-five years of not seeing me but they have been the best few weeks of this old man's life."

"Yes, I have that affect on people." I smiled. "Oh and just for my benefit...exactly how old is my old man?"

"Seven hundred and twenty-two." His lips aimed for a smile but it never made it to his eyes.

"Does that bother you?"

I thought about it. "I don't know yet but that is not nearly as shocking as some of the things I have been subjected to recently." I became silent, just thinking it over. "I really got my work cut out for me though. If crashing on my futon is a highlight for you, then you really have lived a sheltered life." I slowed to stop at a red light and leaned over to kiss his cheek. "I think from now on you are just *Pops* to me. Alexo doesn't seem to fit." I continued on to the yoga studio.

"Yes, undoubtedly the best weeks of my life." He said barely over a whisper.

"Hey, does this mean that I will live as long as you?"

"You are still human so you will still be held to the laws of this world. You probably will have an extended life span, though. Keep yourself safe while I'm gone."

"Sure Pops!" I laughed as he shimmered away.

The closer I got to the studio the more nervous I became. This would be my first test. I had not been around too many people since I came into my Siren abilities. I did not know if I would be able to exercise and concentrate at the same time for at least an hour.

I grabbed my brand new mat and headed towards room number three. I found me a spot in the back and put my mat down. Looking around the room, I found an eclectic mix of people. It was an almost even mix of men and women. At first I was nervous thinking I had signed up for a couple's class but it did not appear that these people were together. It was amusing though. I had pictured a room full of graceful, serious women with color coordinated outfits and mats. This was at least how yoga was seen on TV. I received quite a few overt glances and was truly hoping this did not become a pick up joint.

I snapped out of my reverie when the instructor came in. He was commanding but with a quiet demeanor. He put me in mind of a tall Gandhi. "Welcome to Carl Vegas Studios. I am Carl. Here we will learn breath through poses, meditation through flows and flexibility through concentration. This is not your typical yoga class. We have taken some of the benefits from each type of yoga and blended it together."

He continued to talk but I did not hear any more. I heard my heart beat faster as the most handsome man walked into the class. I generally am not rendered idiotic at the mere sight of a man so I could not understand my reaction. He had light funny colored eyes. They were green, brown and gold. He was tall and lanky in a good way. Trim powerful muscles graced his caramel arms underneath his cut off shirt. This was all I could see before I tore my eyes away.

To make matters worse, he put his mat next to mine and I felt butterflies in my stomach. Imagine that...a grown woman getting butterflies. I felt light headed, giddy like when a stranger buys you a drink at the coffee shop. My reaction to the man was not helping me concentrate. In fact between the heat in the room and him, I could feel my call bubbling up. Carl stopped mid sentence and moved my way. I was beginning to recognize the look he had in his eyes. I closed my eyes and tried to picture a white wall. My breathing started to slow down. At the last minute, Carl veered to the woman next to me and checked her form.

I had been so career focused that when it came to dating I just picked from the pool of men that found me attractive. It was less work to impress them. This has actually worked for me. It was at this moment that I understood that I had been living a half life. I never felt this strong a spark for any of the guys I dated. I never knew I was missing out.

He looked at me and smiled when Carl had motioned for us to pair up for the next portion. "I'm Sahaj. What's your name?" His voice was deep and it complemented his attractiveness.

I knew I had to be grinning like an idiot. This was new territory for me. I managed to eek out a small "Keridan." He made small talk while we went through our poses. I mentally went down the Female's List of Questions...the one we all have when we try to find out more information than we are told. I was elated that we seemed to be hitting it off. I could tell at least there was some interest on his part.

He grabbed my hand to pull the stretch and my mind left the present. I saw a black panther running through the jungle. Something was chasing it. An intense fear hung over the animal. I lost my balance and my concentration which caused me to fall ever so ungracefully. Embarrassed, I jumped up but not before three men rushed over to help me including Sahaj. Controlling this call would be more difficult than I imagined. I felt handicapped by it. I could not express basic emotions without causing a scene.

Carl got the class back focused but not before I

had accumulated a few more admirers. I went back to trying to see my white wall. I could feel despair creeping in. I stole a glance over to Sahaj. He seemed distant now. Whatever progress we were making seemed to be completely shut down now. It is definitely true that the eyes are the windows to your soul. His eyes told me loads.

Class finally ended. I packed slowly hoping I had been wrong about Sahaj. I tried to give him some encouragement to stay and talk. I was no good at these little female ploys. This was definitely foreign territory. He shot me one of those *"As If"* looks before walking out the class. That sealed the deal for me. It was not like I was expecting a marriage proposal but it would have been nice for a number or a *see you next class*. Maybe it was best...I could file him away for one of my future fantasies. At least this way I will never know if he had some disgusting habit that would just ruin those beautiful muscles.

I headed out of the studio to find Sahaj leaning against the wall. Determined to not let this man that I only met ninety minutes ago get to me, I walked right past him without looking his way. I did not get far before he called my name. Maybe I had misinterpreted the signals. My pulse quickened and a knot started to form in my stomach. I took a deep breath and turned around.

In what had to be the most arresting voice I had ever heard he said, "So it starts again."

Confused, I looked up at him. That was a bad idea. His eyes held mine for a brief moment and instant insanity set in. "Pardon?" He walked around me as if assessing the merchandise.

"Oh, do we really need the games? After all this time, I thought we had gotten past this part of our relationship."

He must be delusional. *Well, I guess no one can have it all.* "Look, Sahaj, is it? I'm sorry but a ninety minute aerobics class does not a relationship make, at least not in my world." I tried to keep walking towards my car but he flew back in front of me to block my way. "Seriously, I am hot, tired and really not in the mood for cryptic games from a complete stranger. Maybe we could table this discussion for another time. Let's say, A week from...I don't know...never." I smiled and waited for some response from him.

Nothing - He still blocked my way. I started to feel that he was just more than a little off his rocker.

He started to mumble something in a foreign language and looked intently at me as if he was putting some voodoo curse on me. I shook my head and laughed - one of those deep guttural laughs that you only have after watching a good comedy show on TV. "This has been fun, really. Thanks for ruining a perfectly good fantasy."

There was a look of confusion on his face. I was ecstatic at his reaction. It just was not fair for only me to be the one with absolutely no idea what was going on. While he was momentarily distracted, I did the first thing I could think of. I released my call...hoping that if it worked involuntarily, it would work better when I put some effort behind it.

He instantly became contrite. "Keridan, I must have mistaken you for someone else. Please accept my apologies. Let me make it up to you. Let me buy you some coffee or a car." His wide smile looked cute and boyish like a first crush. He reached out and grabbed my hand. While he looked expectantly for an answer, my mind flew to the same grove my mother had been in before she died and I saw a black panther lounging lazily among the wildflowers.

I snatched my hand away once I flashed back to reality. All my bravado was gone. "Sure, Sahaj, a car is fine." I pushed past him finally, got in my car and headed home.

Chapter 5 – I Mourn For Opportunities Lost

There was no denying that I was angry. As I drove back home I would not let myself digest what had just happened. I was in full adrenaline mode. Two things went through my head playing havoc with my senses – the fact that I could summon my call when needed and the reason I had to do it in the first place. It felt comforting to know that I did have something to defend myself with but I wondered what type of impression it leaves on the person. I decided I needed to talk to the aunties.

After a hot shower, I searched out Aunt Melody. She was the most understanding. I found her in my garden room, which was no more than a bay window with potted plants.

"Am I interrupting?"

She closed her paper and smiled. "No, little one, you are not interrupting me. What can I do for you?" When she spoke my arms tingled. Her voice was like the sound lily petals floating down from the sky – both soft and beautiful.

"So I was at yoga today and there was this guy. At first, I was attracted to him but I got the impression near the end that he was not reciprocating my sentiments. Well, to make a long story short, I cleared my mind and concentrated on him being affected by my call and it worked – really well, in fact. I guess my question in how does this call thing work? What are the consequences? Alexo said it would make me more visible. But how?"

Her ancient eyes flashed from pure light back to regular. "I am glad you are able to exert a little more control over your abilities. How do I explain? Humans have extraordinarily vast amount of untapped brain power. Have you heard of telepathy?" I nodded. I was a trekkie. Any sci-fi fan had. "Well, the Siren's call is a part of this. Your mind is sending out a telepathic signal at all times. Everyone else is just instinctively processing this as an emotion of attraction for you."

"So I am telepathic?"

"No, not like we are. You aren't able to actively send out your thoughts. Your call is about it and it is an involuntary thing for you. This signal also leaves a signature trace that other attuned beings can pick up. The signal hovers around you. The longer you use it, the longer it takes to degrade."

"So when I am concentrating there's no signal floating around me and I look just like any other human? I seem to lose control more often than not, what affect do I have on others? I mean am I sending out some sort of telepathic brain damage? Does the Keridan infatuation imprint something on their brains to just automatically be into me?"

She laughed a little tinkling laugh. "So this is not about the bad guys. I should have known. Honestly! He must have left some impression on you. There is no brain damage but an imprint will be left – more like a warm fuzzy memory."

"So basically, henceforth and forevermore I won't be able to tell if a guy like me for me or because of me. That's just great!"

"Keridan, this may not be the best time for you

to be thinking about a relationship. You are - I mean this with all love - prone to distractions already without any outside influence. It is not like you would be able to be totally honest with the guy. How could you explain why every man in a five mile radius was singularly attracted to you every time he kissed you?" She gave me a hug. I know she meant well but I just could not picture myself a nun.

How much would I be giving up for this new life that landed on my lap? I thought about my previous relationships – all four of them. I stayed in them longer than necessary because it was convenient. I realize now that I probably was not as accessible as I could have been. None of the breakups were heart-stopping-must-eat-chocolate all day. I was however aware that it was me, truly me, that the guys wanted. Be it physical or emotional, it was never against their will or forced unwittingly upon them.

So, that leaves me back at square one. It is ironic that all my super powers revolve around my emotions and because of my emotions I can never be in a relationship. I do not need to be in a relationship to complete me, but I did not want the possibility taken away. There had to be a happy medium somewhere. I had never even considered having a family seriously. That was something people did after thirty.

What could I tell someone if I did try for a relationship? *Guess what, I am not altogether human! Oh yeah, and magic is real.*

It would definitely be a *Bewitched* moment. For now, I guess, it was a mute point. I needed to focus on me...to learn the new me. Some alone time may be the best prescription.

Chapter 6 – Royal Bloodlines

Despite the fact that he was most assuredly a psychopath, Sahaj had a starring role in my dreams. My mind wavered in its new resolve to remain unattached. I thought about him so much that the lines between reality and my fantasy world blurred. I realized that his face, his body became my ideal guy.

I have created this fantasy world in my head that I frequent all the time. Normal Laws of physics do not apply. In fact, before I met my father my fantasy world was the only place where magic was real. Some kids out grew their special imaginary places but I clung to mine with such a vengeance that it stuck – permanently. I have acknowledged that it is the spring where all my creativity comes.

My fantasy world is populated from the remnants of reality. I am very picky who gets to share my mind. With all the unwanted pictures that already clutter my head, I need some space that I can control. Some people obsess over celebrities. They get off on the glamour and beauty. I, on the other hand, have always picked random everyday people to star in my mental movies. It could be the guy at the gas pump right next to me or the UPS delivery man. I think handsome must be a requirement on their application for drivers. I even prefer not talking to them. It generally ruins it for me if I do. This was why it is so shocking that Sahaj had made the cut.

My overactive imagination would be my downfall. It did not help that I worked from home. I am alone most of the time. The only people I have had contact with were my new family and my ever faithful next door neighbor, Robert. He was a literature professor at the state college down the street. He was also a history buff like me so we had an endless amount of things to talk about. I have had to avoid him for the past few weeks. I am sure he thinks it is because of my mom and that I needed some time. It was really because he was secretly in love with me. He does not know *I know* though. He let it slip to my mom once. It just does not seem fair to him to be around me when my call slips.

Robert is the kind of guy that you really wanted to be with. He has the gentleness of a teddy bear and the genteel charm befitting his southern heritage. He was smart and thoughtful but he has never made me feel like Sahaj does. I am really taking this serious. I have developed feelings for a guy that I have only talked to for a couple of hours – even that is stretching it.

Needing to clear my head, I went up to my studio to paint. I looked over my latest pieces and noticed every one was of the panther from my flashes. I picked up a blank sheet and taped it to my easel. I normally worked abstractly but an idea struck me. I began to paint with quick washes the grove that always flew into my head. My father was lying on a hammock so I added him in. I captured as much detail as I could remember.

That night I tried to remember as many flashes from over the past few weeks. There was one of Robert sitting at the airport, Alexo at a waterfall and, of course, the panther. The panther was the most confusing. I was truly baffled by the reasons someone would have a pet panther. Even though I am not an animal person, I could understand the appeal of a cute little kitten as a companion but a big black panther. It was unfathomable.

Morning arrived before I knew it. I had fallen asleep on the floor of my studio. It was Saturday and I had the entire day to myself. All of a sudden, I started to float in the air and twirl. Then Alexo shimmered in up under me.

I giggled like a school girl. "Pops, put me down." His eyes were bright with laughter. He looked to be more like a forty year old model than a several hundred year old Siren. Finally I landed from our air ballet. "When did you get back?"

"Oh, I just got here. I had to see my little girl. I hear you are in love."

"What! No. I have vowed to be a nun just as Aunt Melody suggested. I guess I have to make another vow to never tell Aunt Melody anything again." I pulled a piece of textile from my oriental rug on the floor.

"Don't get too testy." He pointed to his head. "We are all connected you know." He plopped down next to me and glanced around at my paintings.

"You've been busy I see. What's all this?"

"I have been trying to record the things I see in my head...my version of photographic development. Here, see I saw you in this grove." I fingered the painting gently. It was still damp in some places.

"This is a copse from my world. It is amazing that you could capture it so accurately."

"I found it weird you wearing this funny dress but maybe you are a cross-dresser in "Siren Land".

When he did not laugh at my joke, I turned to look at him. His olive colored skin became pasty. "What is it? What did I say?"

"This is bad. I only wear these *robes* when the Council of Sirens meets." He leaned closer.

"When was the last time you met? Why do you have to meet?"

"War. Death. Famine. The last time we wore purple was about sixty or so years ago. I'm willing to bet this is from the future and not the past." I put my arm around his waist and rested my head on his shoulder. "Purple is war."

"There are wars all the time. I'm not being dismissive but what makes sixty years ago different from now?"

"There are wars being fought now between countries – yes. Nations – yes - but not the entire world. We are peace keepers. Once war actually breaks out it takes a lot to diffuse it. When it has gotten to that point, it takes the combined efforts of more than just us. Our world is a symbiotic reality to your world. If something happens that causes calamity on your side it invariably spreads to ours. All those emotions...it burdens us." He took my hand and held it. Then he placed his palm to my palm and mumbled, "*Korshet.*"

I felt an immediate pressure in my hand that traveled up my arm to my head. I heard the ocean like when you listen to a sea shell. The air became thick and it was getting hard to breathe. I started gasping for air. A hundred pounds was sitting on my chest. My mind went dizzy. I could actually see myself still holding Alexo's hand yet I was detached from the whole scene. Hurt. Pain. Love. These emotions washed over me like waves in a fearsome cycle that only grew in intensity.

"*Culpa Mae Shinto.*" Alexo moved his palm from mine and tiny sparks flew between our hands.

"Explain what just happen to me?" The pressure lifted but a dull sound lingered in my ears.

"I made a connection to you – transferring what I thought and felt at the time. The feelings you experienced, were similar to how the human world impacts us. If we are overloaded the pain is intense. The connection is how we Sirens also bond. It allows us to feel and experience what the other has been through...to connect with them on another level."

"What does '*Korshet*' means? What language is it?"

"It was Sirendali, the language of the Sirens. It means *to connect in love* and '*Culpa Mae Shinto*' means *to release in love*. What did you experience? I'm just curious."

"It felt like I had a bad sinus cold. I would get an immense wave of love to come over me. I wanted to go out and hug the world then followed feelings of hurt and pain with equal intensity. I literally watched all this playing out in my head. I was myself but not myself if that makes sense to you."

"Interesting. Your two halves make it work a little different on you. I wonder what happens if you initiated a connection. Try it. Place your palm in mine, think of something you want me to know and say '*Korshet*'."

Still reeling from the last time, I was not anxious

to go again. Reluctantly I did though. Sahaj and Robert flew into my head. I thought of how Alexo has changed my life in such a short time. Of how our relationship is complex but that somehow I now have a lifetime of bonded memories with him. *"Culpa Mae Shinto."*

Alexo grinned like the Cheshire cat. He grabbed me in a big bear hug and spun me around. "Keridan, that was amazing! I couldn't see your pictures, but I could hear you. I could feel you. I share your love."

Our relationship was definitely unusual. He filled a void in my heart more so because I realized that I did not miss out on not having a father growing up. He has given me those years back and more in the short time I have known him. I also now know that I filled a hole in his heart as well.

"Do you have someone special in your realm, like a wife maybe? How was it growing up for you?" We were still sitting on the floor in the studio. Sunlight streamed through the windows and bounced off the many mirrors I had placed in the room. It gave me more natural light for painting.

"No, I have never had a wife. I guess you would call me a confirmed old, *old* bachelor. Sirens live a long time. Our world is structured similarly to yours with some exceptions. Each elemental family has a ruling royal family. They are the delegates from each royal house that are on the Council of Sirens. The Council was the governing body that rules Sirendll. The level of ones abilities is completely controlled by bloodlines. Sirens go off to work everyday just like you except we have no monetary system. No one is working for money. They work for well being."

"Being the son of a princess, I was destined for Council work so I chose to be a peace keeper. I was always focused on doing my job that I never made time for someone else. Time moves differently in Sirendll, our world. We mate differently too. It is actually a science. We must find the one person who we have the strongest connection with. That way any offspring will have the best chance to survive. The elements are part of our very existence. Sirens are born from the link between us and the elements. Some come from the waters: they are the water children. Others come from the land. Still others like me come from the air and clouds. My mother was a sky princess. My abilities – floating and flying – come from her. That is how we all are connected just as the elements are interconnected."

He made a dust bunny from up under my table float up into the air. "So that is why you are always spinning me around. You feel more comfortable in the air."

"No that is just because it makes you laugh. It is amazing. After years of training I went off to help the world. I have spent hundreds of years trying to keep the peace but I have only known peace since you. Having you gave me meaning. You are my soul's completion."

I started to cry. I was glad I still meant the world to someone.

Chapter 7 – Coffee and Competition

I could no longer avoid seeing Robert. I had run out of excuses. Plus, I dearly missed our conversations. I was meeting him at the coffee shop by the university. It was one of those rare days that he had to actually go on campus.

I was reaching for the door when from behind me a voice straight out of my dreams said, "Let me get that for you." I turned to say thanks. "Keridan! I was hoping to run into you again." He gave me a smoldering smile that rendered me senseless...momentarily at least.

"Sahaj, what a surprise." I walked in and stood in line.

"What a *nice* surprise you mean."

"Hmm...That has yet to be seen."

"You are too hard on me. You have been on my mind. I didn't know if you were coming back to yoga. Give a guy some hope. Haven't you thought about me just a little?"

"I must admit I have been thinking about you."

"See, that was easy. Care to share?"

"I was wondering if you were psychotic, neurotic or just your everyday variety of harmless crazy."

"Depending on the day, I might be all three."

I had to laugh. I was being drawn into his charisma. I could feel it. I had to back away and come up for air. This was definitely not the path to nun-hood. I ordered my coffee and searched for a spot to sit. Being so close to the college, this was a hot spot for the hanging out crowd. I went for the love seat in the back. Sahaj followed.

"So what do I need to convince you that I am not as bad as you may think? How can I get into your good graces? Flowers? Chocolates? Candy?"

"That wouldn't get you very far with me."

"How about a lifetime of servitude? I am very

good with my hands." He rubbed his finger along the side of my hand just barely making contact.

I moved my hand to abate the tingling sensation left by his touch. "Not necessary. The last thing I need is more undying servitude."

"Oh, so there is a line forming already. Better for me. I always like a challenge especially when you are the prize."

"Sahaj, help me out here - last week I was some kind of pariah to you and now...not so much. Trust me; I am not complaining but what gives?"

"You have caught my attention."

"Hmm...I have caught your attention. If nothing else, that's a first." My favorite panther flashed into my head. He was walking near the edge of a forest. I shook out of my daydream. Now was not the time. "Do you have a pet? Maybe a cat?" It can not be a coincidence that my panther pops into my head when Sahaj is around.

"Maybe a cat." He seemed to answer with a little less confidence but no less cocky.

Before I could get a better explanation, I saw Robert walk in. He approached us warily. Sahaj looked briefly at him. "So this is contestant number two?"

Robert came over and gave me a hug and kissed my cheek. In his adorable country accent he said, "Keri-*Darling*." That was what he called me. According to him the *d-a-n* in my name did not suit my personality. "Sorry, I'm late."

"No worries. Robert this is Sahaj. Sahaj, Robert. Sahaj is in my yoga class."

Robert's vanilla soy milk complexion contrasted sharply to Sahaj's coffee with cream one as they shook hands. Robert was on his guard. I could tell. Sahaj seemed to be enjoying himself.

"Keridan, I'll leave you to your company. See you in class." He smirked a bit. Then out of the blue he leaned in a kissed my cheek as well. There was no fireworks like there had been in my fantasies but I did have to briefly close my eyes. Faster than humanly possible, he was gone. Maybe it just seemed that time had stopped.

I opened my eyes to meet Robert's. There was alarm in his eyes but he held his peace.

"New admirer?"

"I don't really know what he is. It doesn't matter. I have resolved to grow to be an old maid.

Relationships at this point would further complicate my life." I looked towards the direction that Sahaj had left then moved over so Robert could sit next to me in the overstuffed seat. He still was agitated. "So what has been going on with you for the past few weeks?"

"Before that..." He wrapped his arm around mine. "How have you been? I was getting worried about you. You haven't really surfaced since your mom passed."

"I actually am good. My mom is kind of still taking care of me." I told him about how she introduced me to my father and aunts. I left out the super natural part. I explained how we had just been having a small family reunion over the past few weeks.

"So back to you... How's the book coming?"

"Oh! Keri-Darling. I am so excited. I'm going to India. I was awarded a small grant to finish my research." *That would explain why I saw him at the airport,* I thought to myself. Robert was writing a book on legends and myths surrounding tribes indigenous to India and Africa over the past few centuries. "I've found some really old tribes that have had little contact with the modern world. I'm working on getting a guide to take me in the jungle."

"That's great! Hey, why don't you come over in a few days and let me cook you dinner to celebrate. You can meet my new family."

"Mash potatoes and gravy?"

"With chicken, biscuits and apple pie."

"I am so there."

We talked for a couple of hours. I was proud of myself for being able to control my call for so long. Alexo would be proud. The sky was turning a pinkish orange which meant it was time to go. "Ok, Mr. Professor, you have some *younglings* to go educate."

"Don't remind me. They seem to get younger every year. And of course they already know everything." I sat up on the sofa to pull him up but he just pulled me back into his chest. "That's better. I think I'll ditch today."

"Then you will be ditching by yourself. I have to go. I punched him on the shoulder. He grabbed my hand and wanted to say something but did not. He just rubbed little circles into the back of my hand. "Come on. You can walk me to my car." I was starting to recognize the look from his eyes.

We walked silently to the car. His naturally playful demeanor did not return. There was a wall of unspoken words building between us as tall as the tallest edifice in the Atlanta skyline. I was sure I was blocking the *love signals* from leaving my head. This conversation would just have to wait until he got ready to say what he needed to say out loud.

It was impossible to not compare the mysterious Sahaj against the dependable Robert during my drive back to the house. Robert has had plenty of women beating down his door. He was a charmer; but for every woman that he introduced me to I could not see him through their eyes. The way they looked at him. I can tell when he is interested in them. He wears burnt orange. I had told him once how nice he looked in the color once – how it complemented the light glints in his hair. I think he went out and bought an entire mall's worth of clothes in that color. He wears it generally only for me so he really likes someone when he pulls it out for someone else.

Now when I see Sahaj enter a room, every woman in the room sneaks a peak – a lot of men too, this is Atlanta after all. I can see what is on their minds because it is on mine as well. Maybe there was something in our make up that subconsciously draws us to a person even against our own wishes. I hoped not.

Chapter 8 – Friends Don't Let Friends Bowl Mad

Alexo was desperately trying to distract me from painting. He had been putting me through my paces for the past few days. I needed a break. I worked most of the day at my job then painted for the rest of the night. I could see out the corner of my eye that he was pouting.

"I thought children were supposed to listen to their parents."

"Maybe where you come from."

"Keridan!"

"Just give me tonight to be human. In fact, I have an idea. Tonight you are going to be at my mercy." I put my brush down, reached around and yanked him up. "All work and no play makes for a very irritable Keridan."

Alexo followed me out to my car. "So, where are you taking me...against my will, might I add?"

"We are going bowling. I need some clean, mind-numbing American fun."

Pure light flashed from his eyes. "Bowling!"

"What's wrong with bowling? If you want a happy, willing Keridan, then you will wear some ugly, used shoes and throw a ball at some unsuspecting pins."

"Manipulating, human female!"

"And proud of it!"

We arrived at the bowling alley which was crowded as usual. We picked our number and sat at the table to wait to be called. I ordered some food. Shortly after that, the waitress brought out our nachos with jalapenos. She nearly swooned when Alexo thanked her.

"Now, who can't control themselves? You are going to make these women faint. Have a nacho."

"That's not me. *I* can control myself."

"Well don't look at me. She definitely had eyes

for you."

"I am charming."

"If you do say so yourself."

"I've never been bowling before. Is this supposed to be fun?"

"Yes it is. How can you have lived for centuries and never been bowling?"

"I use to peek in on you and your mom but I have never had the need. When I am in this realm it is generally to work or more recently to see you. You seem to really love nachos!"

He pointed to the near empty bowl in front of me. I had gorged myself. Nachos and cheese was right up there with ice cream in the way of comfort foods for me. "I only get to have them at sporting events. You can say it is just a tradition. You seem very impatient today. This is supposed to be relaxing. So relax."

"Hmm." He turned to the counter and smiled at the lady working the register. She blinked and then called our number. Next six of the ten lanes abruptly ended their games. By the time we made it up to the front desk, the once crowded ally was nearly empty.

"What did you just do?"

He smiled. "Just keeping the peace - the peace between you and me at least."

"Do you do that often – just make people do whatever you want?"

"Yes."

"Have you ever done that on me?"

"Trust me, it doesn't work on you."

"You've tried!"

"Of course I have. You can be very stubborn at times." He motioned to the bowling alley as if I should understand.

I was becoming angry. This was supposed to be fun and relaxing however Alexo was not cooperating. I normally can control my temper but it is getting harder and harder. This was the first time since I had known him that Alexo was visibly upset with me. As we walked to our lane, we passed a small family. All of a sudden the parents started to yell at the kids and each other. I looked at Alexo who seemed just as shocked as I was. The couple in the next lane started shouting as well.

Alexo laughed. "Unbelievable."

"What now!" I just snapped.

"I can feel your anger. You don't need to yell.

You really need to calm down before we get in the middle of a brawl." He motioned to the rest of the bowling alley. Just about everyone in the place was involved in some sort of altercation. "You are projecting your emotions."

"That's just great! Can't be in love. Can't get angry. What next!" I plopped down on the hard plastic seats dejected.

He sat next to me and rubbed my shoulders. "I know I push you too hard but with all these disappearances I want you to be as prepared as you can be. This is new for you. I have imposed myself on you in the most unimaginable ways. You have to accept the existence of another world, a new father, and new abilities. To top it all off, everyday your life is in danger from some unknown force."

He placed his palm on my palm. I knew what was coming next. I heard the ocean again but this time there was not any pain. I was sitting in a beach chair lounging under a blue canvas umbrella. A bird in the sky circled lowly and landed on a dry piece of driftwood that jutted above the white powder sand bank. Behind me was a row of beach houses. A nice looking man ran casually near the edge of the tide water. He stretched then looked strangely at me.

Walking up, he introduced himself as Teranodor. I knew he was a Siren because his eyes flashed pure light as he spoke. Sitting down beside me, he became quiet. We both just stared out at the blue-green ocean. I became lost in the sounds of waves crashing into the sand and receding back into the ocean.

When I was released from the connection, every person in the bowling alley seemed back to normal. Even I was not as angry as before. We only played one game. My heart was not in it. I guess it was going to take just a little more to get me out of my funk.

We headed back to the house. Alexo stayed with me every night but Aunt Melody, Eiliel and Adiron took turns. Tonight however no one was at the house when we returned. Alexo followed me into the kitchen. He and I were getting more attuned to each other emotions. His ancient eyes looked their age for a brief moment. I felt ashamed. I could recognize that I acted terrible this evening. Realizing this made the hurt feel even worse. I knew better than to act like a petulant child but this temper is getting the best of me. I went over to him and folded myself into his arms and whispered, "Sorry." His soft cottony dreadlocks tickled my ears.

"I will try to find a way to make it better for you."

I went upstairs to shower and get ready for bed. When I came back downstairs for something to drink, he was gone. There was no note but somehow I knew he would not be here tonight. Accepting this made me feel more alone than ever. That was the first night the nightmares came.

Chapter 9 – I See Kidnapped People

Distant drums were beating an anonymous melody as I was running through the jungle. I was being hunted. Animal after animal made vain attempts to slow down the woman on my behalf. She was exquisitely dark skinned with ancient markings on her arms and hands. Tree branches scratched at my arms while the humidity in the air settled on my skin. I knew I had to protect someone but their face was just past my line of recognition. She drew her bow about to strike when a black panther leapt over my head to put itself between us. Instead of a roar, a human voice came out of its mouth saying, "Keridan, I wanted to personally congratulate you on a job well done."

I was definitely dreaming. My answering machine was blinking red. Sweat was pouring from my face. My bed looked as if it was on the losing side of a war. I first picked up my sketch book by the bed and tried to remember the markings on the woman's arms from my dreams. I sketched as much as I could remember before it started to get fuzzy. The clock said seven thirty. I pushed the button on the machine to listen to the entire message. My boss was all animated. "Keridan, I wanted to personally congratulate you for a job well done. Six weeks ahead of schedule and twenty-five thousand dollars under budget. Enjoy six weeks vacation all paid with a bonus."

It was a very strange message and way too much to process before coffee. Picking up the phone, I headed downstairs. Sitting at the island in the kitchen was Alexo. "Morning, I thought I wasn't going to see you for a while. Sorry about last night." I went over and gave him a big hug.

"Morning back. I needed to take care of a few things. Eat up. We have a long day."

"I need to call my boss. He left me a weird message this morning."

"No need. I thought you needed a break so I made it so you could get one. You seem bent on trying to do everything at one time."

I knew I should have been angry. This was my career, my life. I should get some say in how it goes. I however, felt relieved. I could not begin to understand how he was able to convince all the stakeholders that my project was completed, but I was not going to look a gift horse in the mouth. "That was very thoughtful of you. Unnecessary, but thoughtful. Hey what is that thing you are doing with your hands? I've seen it before." I started to peel apples for tonight's dinner with Robert.

"I was trying to remember a symbol." He motioned to the counter top. "This was the pattern." He traced with his fingers what looked like Sanskrit.

"Wait a sec." I ran upstairs and picked up the drawing I did this morning. "Look, this is similar." He fingered the drawing. "Last night I had a nightmare. When I woke up, I was able to remember this sign. The woman chasing me wore this." He absentmindedly started rubbing my back. I could feel a sensation in my head. Pressure was being released. "You are doing some voodoo on me again."

Alexo looked from his hand to me. "It helps

with nightmares. I need to go to the archives to find out more on this symbol." He stole a couple apple slices.

I popped him over the knuckles. "Wait for dinner." He shimmered back and forth to my apple bowl so quickly he seemed to be just a blur. "What are you like two years old? I'm not going to have enough for my pie." Alexo put on a boyish pout.

He started back going over the drawings. "Hey, do you know someone named Teranodor?"

"Where did you here that name from?"

"He was with me when you made the connection with me at the bowling alley. He looked like a Siren...pointy ears, flashing eyes. He didn't say much."

Faster than imaginable, Alexo whirled me around causing me to drop my knife and apples to the floor. "Describe him exactly." His eyes turned to light. This time however they did not flash back to normal. I describe him to the best of my abilities. He slowly put me down, pinched his nose and let out a soft screech like a bird chirp. My aunts shimmered in. I was getting anxious now.

He turned to Melody. "She saw him. She saw

Teranodor."

A faint blush flitted across her cheeks. In her tinkling voice she asked, "How? Her visions are only based on people she knows or has a relationship with."

"By the looks on your faces, I can tell this means something. Could you perhaps clue me in?"

"Teranodor was to be your aunt's mate but he was one of the first to disappear. You being able to see him, talk to him, well it is hope." We need to know if you are able to communicate with him actually or is it some kind of illusion." He held his palm out for me to connect with it. "If you see him ask about," he turned to Melody and she nodded slightly, "the field of pearls."

We made the connection and I was back sitting on the beach with the sounds of the ocean lulling in my ears. Three men were running towards me. Teranodor was one of them. He sat beside me again. The other two knelt in front of me looking on curious. I turned to Teranodor. "Can you tell me about the field of pearls?"

He cocked his head slightly. His motions were detached and slow as if he was moving under water. "How can this be? Do you know me?"

"I am learning of you."

He touched my arm and little sparks flew off an invisible barrier that flew up between us. "The field of pearls is a special place. It is where dreams begin."

"Why can't we find you? Where are you hidden?"

"My eyes are closed. My thoughts have been silenced. There are great machines to lock my mind. There are many of us. This is Eriben and Nastra." He pointed to the other men. "Are you a searcher?"

"No. I am just a friend...Just Keridan. I wish to help."

"We need to find the searchers. We need to warn them." He looked imploringly. He let out a scream and the three mean slowly faded."

I woke up in Alexo's arm with concern all over his face. I must have passed out. I have had a bad case of syncope my entire life but it seems in the last few weeks it has roared its ugly head too many times. I got up slowly. "How long was I out?"

"Not too long. Take it slow. What happened?"

"Ouch!" The room started to spin. I went back down to Alexo's lap. I told them about the searchers and the barrier. I drunk a little juice that Aunt Eiliel brought me. I was able to sit up this time. "Why does it hurt so badly this time?"

"I think the connection is actually being hijacked in some way. I wasn't thinking about Eriben or Nastra. Whatever is blocking their telepathic communications to other Sirens is coming through to you. We need to talk with the council." He looked to Aunt Adiron who promptly sat by my side and rubbed my back. It was the same motion Alexo used to soothe me after my nightmares. "Adiron will stay with you."

"Don't forget about dinner tonight with Robert."

He kissed my cheek. "I won't."

"Remember, no flying or eye flashing or anything remotely non human."

Laughing he said, "I'll be on my best behavior."

Chapter 10 – I Played At The Park

Aunt Adiron helped me get dinner started. She had an unhealthy fascination with TV cooking shows. My simple dinner was heading towards a seven course meal. She watched everything while I got ready for yoga. I took extra care getting ready. I knew the only reason was Sahaj. It was a weakness. Just being present in his company caused me to take extra care ensuring my hair was perfect. My resolve to not be with a man had become just empty promises when I thought about him.

Kissing my aunt, I headed off to class. Arriving too early gave me an excuse to calm down. I put on my headphones and listened to some Abbey Lincoln.

After a few minutes there was a knock on my window. Opening my eyes, I saw Sahaj standing there smiling brilliantly. His muscles were exaggerated by the cut of the shirt. Deltoids, triceps, biceps all bulged seemingly welcoming me into his arms. Slowly, I got out my car.

"You look exhausted!" My little world started to deflate – sound effects and all. I mentally started chastising myself for letting my mind let me get this far. I had to somehow rein in my common sense.

"Gee, thanks. That's what every woman wants to hear." I moved at normal speed now, hurrying towards the door.

He grabbed my hands and spun me around. "That was concern...not criticism. There is a difference." No taunting did I detect from his eyes. I was left to wonder wear my tough skin had went. "How about we do something to help you relax?"

"Isn't that why I came to yoga?"

Still clutching my fingers he pulled me closer to him then lead me in the opposite direction of the studio. He came to a stop. "A motorcycle! No, I don't do motorcycles. Fast. Reckless. No air bags. *BUGS!*"

He had his arm around my waist before I could get too far away. "Don't you trust me?"

"Not *that* much." I pointed to the bike to make my point.

"Hmmm. Well we'll have to work on your trust issues." He reached over the bike and unhooked a saddle bag then threw it over his chest. A man-made lake lined with dogwood trees was nestled below the back of the studio. A park was off to the side. Not a lot of kids were out yet. School was still in. We meandered our way to the two-seater swing.

It was actually very calming to just swing back and forth. Blooming trees, pollen and fragrant flowers smells wafted through the air. The swings were set high enough that even my long legs did not touch the ground. Sahaj was wearing an earthy smelling cologne. That was a point in his favor. I hated men who wore spicy scents. I was a self proclaimed expert on men's cologne as it was all that I wore. Ladies perfume always smelled too sweet to me.

"So what is this all about? Did you just want a ditch day?"

"You don't seem to know how to relax." His head was resting on the chains of the swing. He opened one eye and peeped over at me.

"And you are going to teach me how, I presume."

"Among other things...*if* you like."

I ignored that comment. "Are you some knight in shining armor going around the city making sure random women are happy enough?"

"Not random women. I don't have that much time on my hands."

"I must have just lucked out today."

"Well, I am applying for a permanent position. You should put in a good word for me."

"You flirt as easy as you breathe."

"Actually, I'm a bit out of practice." He pushed one leg lazily off the ground so the swing could pick up momentum.

"So what should I know about you? Give me your story...the short version. I do have somewhere to be this evening."

"Short version. I'm an outdoor person. I prefer to be in the elements than inside. I have lived all over the world which gives me a different perspective on things. I love oranges and mangoes. I was an environmentalist before it was popular." He leaned over and whispered, "My secret obsession is gummy bears."

"Gummy bears! What are you, twelve?"

"Hey, don't knock the gummy bears." I swear a little twinkling lights bounced off his teeth just like in the toothpaste commercials. "What about Keridan? What's underneath the beauty and mystery?" He nudged my shoulder a little.

"I'm not an outdoor person. Let me rephrase. I like parks, mountains that kind of outdoors especially when it is accompanied by a nice condo. I'm not the camping and fishing type of girl. I love to paint, anything artsy actually. My favorite fruits are pineapple and grapefruit. I don't think I have a secret obsession. If I like something, I feel I am pretty much entitled to like it."

"So what are your plans for tonight?"

"I'm having a celebration dinner for my friend Robert."

"Ah, yes, contestant number two. What are we celebrating?"

I rolled my eyes. "It's not like that with Robert or anyone for that matter. He is writing a book and he won a grant to continue his research. So we are just getting together to celebrate. In fact, it is nothing extraordinarily different than any other the Friday night."

"Sounds positively exciting!" He put on the best self-important look he could muster.

"Stop that. Play nice."

"Alright. So when should I arrive?"

"Since when were you invited?"

"I don't need an invitation. You would have thought all the ride home of how you could have asked me over. Then when you got home you would have berated yourself even further wondering what would happen if I just showed up at your front door. I really am trying to help you out."

"Wow, is there any room left on your planet to live or does you big head take up the whole thing?"

He picked up my fingers and kissed them one at a time. "There is always room for you in my world."

I could get use to this. I could get use to him. Sahaj was dangerous to my will power. He said things I did not even know I wanted to hear.

He continued to tell me stories about himself. He was unbelievably easy to be around. After a while even his easy going flirtation changed into just a friendly banter. It was like he was just happy to be around me. He seemed starved for human contact. While talking, he played with my hair or the tag of my shirt – just some small contact.

It became clear that Sahaj was breaking down the common sense barriers I placed in my mind. I had to limit exposure before I ended up at a point where I had to lie about who I was.

I scooted to the edge of the swing surprised that so much time had past. "Thanks for my relaxing afternoon. It was just what the doctor ordered." I stood up and stretched. "I guess I will see you around."

He looked like a hurt little child. "That sounds oddly like a goodbye. I have waited for such a long time to find you. I'm not just letting you walk away."

"It's not goodbye...just a not right now. My life is complicated right now – more so than you can imagine."

"We can make a list of his and her hard times and compare. This afternoon was nice. We have something. I can tell you feel it also. Your heart has an extra beat just for me."

"This was nice. I can admit that. I have no problem with being friends just nothing more. We haven't known each other long enough to profess anything other than infatuation." I tried to lighten the mood. "Besides, I haven't ruled out the fact that you are some crazy sociopath."

"No, I just know what I want. There is no need to put off the inevitable."

"Well, how about this, I know what I want and that is to not make my life any more difficult than it already is."

"I am a patient man." He grabbed my hand and walked silently back to my car. Before I opened my door he leaned over and gave me a hug. "I love the smell of your hair." He reluctantly let me go, looked me up and down and then cupped my chin. Inches away from my lips he whispered, "See you around."

Chapter 11 - Party Crasher

Alexo was poring over some papers when I got home. He looked up long enough to smile and motioned me over. "How was your council session?"

"It's still going on. I came back for dinner. You've given us a little hope."

"I'm glad that I can help in some way."

He patted my hand. "You are extraordinary. No matter what, please remember that."

I kissed his forehead then headed upstairs to take a shower before Robert arrived. This had been a long, interesting day. Sahaj was right about one thing. I did wonder what would happen if I had invited him over. My heart and head were at war. The door bell sounded below. I dashed downstairs. Alexo met me at the door and draped his arm around my waist. My mom always did the same thing. It still amazes me that he was there for all the moments in my life...even the little unimportant ones.

"Robert, this is my father Alexo."

"Pleased to meet you."

I moved out of the way and Robert went over to the chair he liked to sit in. The tail part of his shirt hung out his pants which made him look like an overgrown third grader. You just had to love him. He was adorable.

Alexo knew him of course however he was very convincing otherwise. They quickly became engrossed talking about his research. Robert stood up when I walked in the room. He was always the gentlemen.

"Keri-darling, is there anything you need me to do?"

"No, the food will be out in a minute."

My mom and I would love to give parties. She had this thing about not sitting at a table to eat. In fact, she never owned a dining set. She would place food throughout the room on these little pedestals. Dinners would be a buffet style cornucopia every night. She did it even if she ate alone. It has kind of stuck with me. I called everyone in for dinner and notice as per usual Robert was barefoot.

"Where are your shoes this time?"

"Oh, probably still in the backyard. I am going to have to remember to just leave some shoes over here in the future."

Laughing, I said, "You need a keeper."

"Yes, I know. I already have someone in mind." He moved closer to me just as I went to get some cups off the counter. This knocked off a barrage of papers off the counter that Alexo had left there earlier. Robert picked up the stack, glancing briefly at the sketches. "Keri-darling, are you learning a new language?"

"Not that I am aware of, why?"

"This just looks like some symbols I have come across." He held up the lettering from my dream hunter.

"Really! Hold that thought." I got Alexo's attention and motioned him over. "My father would love to hear about this." Alexo glided over holding his apple pie.

He pointed to a curve in the symbol. "You see here. It looks like an older form of one of the

Dravidian dialects maybe from southern India. I have been brushing up on some of these older languages for my trip." He put the sheet down and got him some dessert.

Alexo was quiet. He had his lost-in-thought look on. The phone and the door rang at the same time. Robert went to get the door while I went into the other room to get the phone. It turned out to be one of those annoying surveys. Even after being polite as possible it takes a while to get them off the line.

Walking back to the kitchen, I was shocked to see Sahaj standing there holding a fruit bouquet of pineapples and grapefruit. He looked sheepish and beautiful at the same time. His smile filled the entire room. My feet would not move any further into the room. All normal reactions were usurped by my own elation of him going through the trouble of finding me. All eyes were on me but I literally could not talk. Robert looked mad. Alexo stunned. The aunts looked resigned.

Coming to my rescue, Alexo jumped up. "Keridan, would you be mad if I stole Robert away for a while." Robert was a little stunned by this request but quickly seemed engaged in the idea of leaving. I shook my head no. Robert had a kind of dazed look and I suspected Alexo was messing with his mind. "Robert, I would really like you to show me more about those symbols." Alexo lean over and kissed my forehead then whispered, "I'm taking the pie." With that he and Robert left to go next door.

"Sahaj what are you doing here?" The aunts quietly slipped out of the room.

"I told you I was coming over. Look, I even brought dessert." He smiled. I frowned. "Now this is the part where you say *'Welcome to my home'* and then you show me around."

"Okay, let me try this again. How did you know where to find me? Are you stalking me now?"

He patted his nose. "No, I know people." He then came over and gave me a big hug lifting me a foot off the ground.

Wanting him was bad enough but having him so near was torture. He was like the best oatmeal raisin cookie that was sitting on a shelf just out of reach. If I was truly honest with myself, I was beyond attracted to him and he seemed to be in to me but I knew deep down that it was not real. He lifted my face to his and looked down at me, "Is having me here really so bad?"

"Honestly, it's a little freaky but since you did bring me grapefruit I'll try to be a better host."

I told him to make himself a plate while I found my aunts. Apparently, they were waiting for me just outside in the hall. It felt like I was a little kid who just got caught sneaking a boy in the house. Aunt Melody opened her mouth to say something but I stopped her. "It's not like I told him to come here. Just come meet him." Their eyes flashed to light and I knew they were talking telepathically behind my back or rather in front of my face. I threw up my hands in surrender.

I introduced Sahaj to my aunts. If there ever was a time I wished I was telepathic it was in that very moment. He seemed to be completely charmed by them. Their call must have a different affect on people than mine. After excusing themselves, I could hear peals of laughter coming from the other room. I felt like their life-sized baby doll.

Turning my thoughts back to Sahaj, I could not help but admire his eyes. Sometimes he looked like a scruffy little kid. I think I must just be attracted to the boyish type. He entwined his fingers in mine and pulled me closer to himself. Who could resist this feeling?

"So, am I forgiven for barging in on your little party?"

"No. I don't think you understand the concept of *Not Right Now.*"

"Technically, you said that this afternoon. Currently, this is a different time frame." When he smiled a dimple appeared on his lower lip. He ran a finger down the base of my neck then pulled me into his arms so I could be nestled against his chest.

We were outside the lower level of my studio. When I first bought this house I converted this big unusable space into my art studio. The room had an open floor plan with the upstairs loft portion being my painting space. The downstairs functioned as my own gallery. He buried his face in my hair as we walked inside.

Sahaj suddenly became rigid and quiet as he looked around the room. I looked over my shoulder at him. "What's wrong?"

He spun me around and looked at me a long time. He seemed to be searching for something in my face. Pointing to the wall only one word came out. "Panther."

"Oh. I have a sudden fascination with panthers

at the moment. I feel very connected to this black one."

A throaty rumble came from Sahaj. He started mumbling to himself. "What are you doing? OK, the crazy guy is back." With my hand on my hip, I started fidgeting.

"Keridan, you're killing me!"

"What!"

"If this is how I am to go then let me have something to remember." With that he grabbed both of my arms and began to kiss me. Softly at first then with such intensity we seemed to become one person. I melted into his body. He placed a trail of kisses down my jaw line then on to my collarbone. I was so lost I did not even realize I was being lifted off the ground by at least twelve inches. Sahaj had picked me up with only one hand. His free hand ran down my leg and softly cupped my bottom. He moaned, swung me gently and cradled me in his arms. With his lips never leaving mine, he gently sat me on the stair case. He knelt in front of me. "I am completely under your spell." Though passion was still in his eyes they were tinged with a little sadness.

I leaned back on the steps and closed my eyes trying to catch my breath and my sanity. His kisses left me incoherent. Little waves of desire rippled through me. Through the haze in my head I heard him say, "Now we can begin." When I looked up however all that was there was the big black panther from my dreams.

Chapter 12 – What Are You?

After all the abnormal things that have happened to me lately, you would think that I would be able to handle weird situations well. Having not come down from my kissing high and looking directly into the face of a ravenous beast, there was really only one thing to do – Scream! I scrambled up to my feet, stumbled up the stairs until I reached the landing. My heart was racing, this time with fear instead of passion. Past nightmares resembled current realities. Alexo and his sisters shimmered in front of me forming a protective circle around me. There features were hard and frightening but no less beautiful.

The panther cocked his head and circled the base of the stairs. On his return trip he just lay down and licked his paws. Alexo relaxed his stance, approached the panther and patted his head.

"I'm guessing you worked your infamous head trick." I stayed behind Alexo. "We need to find Sahaj. He was here before the panther showed up." I looked down and the panther and his greenish eyes looked back at me. At that moment it hit me like a ton of bricks. "Alexo, do all mythical creatures really exist? I've been having dreams about a black panther...this black panther. Either my dreams are manifesting into reality or…" my voice trailed off as the panther morphed into Sahaj.

Dumbstruck, we all just looked at Sahaj who in turn pierced his eyes only on me. "How much bizarre stuff can happen to me in a given month?" I looked Alexo. "No offense."

Alexo walked up to Sahaj. "You're an *animorphii*. Fascinating!"

Incredulous! "Fascinating? Alexo, really?"

Aunt Melody chimed in. "Keridan, hold your temper. I think there is a story we need to hear." She motioned toward Sahaj.

Sahaj walked towards me but was intercepted by my family. He threw up his hands. "Keridan, I would never hurt you. In fact, I thought it was you trying to hurt me?"

Thinking back to the previous moments we shared, I was truly confused. "How, pray tell, did you come to that conclusion?"

He looked up to the ceiling. "The short version...I am eternally hunted by one soul - one soul who will be irresistible to me. This huntress will have the ability to not only wound me but devastate this world." He took a deep breath. "Keridan, you have been wreaking havoc on me since the day we met. I come to your house and see paintings of *me* on your wall. What else am I to think?"

A small part of me was overjoyed. This beautiful man admitted to me and my family that he wanted me. This man was also a strange shape shifting cat. That aside, I am part Siren which basically means he could not help himself in the wanting department. That thought quickly washed cold water on my feelings. "Who are you?"

"I am Sampoerna Ade Sahaj, son of Rachmad Ramelan and Nairi Dewi, crown prince of the Puhave Empire at your service." He bowed towards me.

"That was a mouthful. What do you mean crown prince?"

"Many years ago, half a world away was my country. The Puhave Empire consisted of a few islands in the Indian Ocean west of what is now considered Indonesia. We were a small sea-faring society. We were on the brink of joining our country with the neighboring kingdom of Mahera when the unthinkable happened. A great wave came on our lands which made it sink to the bottom of the ocean. A few survivors finally made it to Tamil Nadu."

"I missing the part where you become a panther and I'm suppose to hurt you." He looked positively uncomfortable. He curled up on one of the floor pillows. Unconsciously, we all leaned forward and sat down as well.

"The joining of Puhave and Mahera was to be sealed by the marriage of myself and Princess Ida. A small sect of priests from Mahera opposed the joining. They insisted that we of Puhave were ruining the souls that lived in the waters around us. They practiced at type of animism. Their priests were what you may call Shamans. They at first cursed me to be a panther hoping that would be enough to stop the union; however, they did not account for Princess Ida actually loving me even though our marriage was arranged. As a high priestess, she used her powers to give me the ability to change between forms. This outraged the priests who in turned cursed Princess Ida. Her soul was forced to forever search, to be drawn to me, to love me completely and inexplicably but at a price. As soon as a connection is made between our souls, she is programmed to kill me. She has these arrows that are imbued with pieces of her soul. They can kill me in human form only. If I am wounded catastrophe happens. That is what happened to my country." He pointed to a tiny mark just below his collarbone. "A great earthquake shook beneath the volcano Krakatau, followed by a tsunami."

Attempting to process all that he said, I stood and approached Sahaj. An overwhelming need to protect him, comfort him overtook me. I had eighty thousand questions in my head. I could sympathize even empathize with him. Being part Siren, it was hard for me to trust love but to be cursed to harm your true love for an eternity was a tough realization to face. I looked back to Alexo. He nodded his understanding. Quietly, he and my aunts left the room. Seeing that they can read minds and had supersonic hearing, it was the gesture that counted.

"I don't know if you will believe me but there is no way I am the Princess Ida from your story. Trust me."

"Princess Ida's soul is reincarnated after every attempt on my life."

"I don't really believe in reincarnation."

He grabbed my hands and pulled me closer to his side. "Just because *you* don't believe in something doesn't make it less real." That glorious smiled framed his shining white teeth briefly.

I shifted a little so I would not get sucked into his brilliance. "How long has this been going on? I'm a history buff and I have never heard of Puhave. I have heard of Krakatau though."

"Well, I am a little older than I look."

"That's not so strange in my world. What am I looking at...give me a ball-park figure?"

"I was born around 1650. Somehow the curse has given me a long life. Princess Ida's curse however takes away life, love and death. What they did to her was more than anyone soul should have to bear. I never know who she will be or when she will show up in my life. I just will be completely drawn to her." He rubbed the back of my hand. He seemed to be speaking more to himself than to me. "You are her. The trigger just has not happened yet."

"If what you say is true, big on the *if,* I am not her. I am, though, curious as to why tell me all this? Why show me the panther side at all?"

"I am constantly on guard for Princess Ida which causes me to move around a lot. It's harder for her to find me as a panther so in the early years I was a panther most of the time. Life didn't really matter to me after so much devastation. The priests got their wish and more. I had no country, no family, no Ida. I roamed the jungle lands of Sri Lanka and Tamil Nadu. I have hunted in Africa, Asia and Australia. It was a peaceful century but my humanity slowly resurrected and so did the battles between me and Ida." He paused to face me. "My attraction for you is so strong that I am willing to obliterate the south eastern seaboard for just one of your kisses." He leaned in to kiss me again but I stopped him. As wonderful as his kisses are and I did mean wonderful, I was not so confused to think that this could continue.

"Sahaj, I am not your one. I know this may seem

like a blow to you ego but I don't love you. I do like you, probably more than I will admit to under normal circumstances. I know the difference. I can live without you." He was not fazed by my declaration. "This strong attraction you have for me is not real. I'm pretty much made for you to like me. That is just a part of who I am. You see, I am a Siren." He looked confused. "Let me see how to better explain this to you. Let me show you." I had been practicing so much lately I could control even the level of intensity of my call. Standing up, I walked across the room. "Now, I want you to try your hardest to stay where you are sitting." I released my call full force. He nearly broke his neck running over to me. He started kissing the palms of my hands. I stopped him and myself. "See you can't help yourself." I moved away disgusted. "When you are around me you will have no more control over how you think you feel for me than I do when I unconsciously broadcast them."

"Great!" He wrapped his arms around my waist. "So we are just two supernatural freaks of nature." This did not comfort me. "It's been hundreds of years, literally, since I have felt this way about someone. I don't care what you are. I don't even care what I am. I just need to be around you."

"Well, it matters to me. I still have a choice."

"I would never take your choices away. I just want you to give me a chance. You like me. I like you. You have some weird mind trip and I happen to be an over sized house cat. What two people could be more perfect for each other?"

I let out a huge frustrated sigh. Alexo shimmered in behind Sahaj. "Everything okay?" He draped his arm over my shoulder.

"No!" I nearly shouted his head off.

He started his back-rub-to-calm-me down move. I have started to recognize his technique to temper my temper. It was working but not fast enough. I looked down to my imaginary watch. "Whew, look at the time. I think I have had enough excitement for one day. Alexo is hardly able to contain himself. He has on his million-question face." I braved a look to Sahaj. "Do you mind?"

"Anything for you Keridan." He bowed slightly. Dimples appeared on Alexo's delighted face. I left the two of them and walked in search of a quiet place to think.

Meandering through the house, I would hear the

occasional footfall behind me. My aunts would each in turn look at me, concern etched in their faces. For the most part, though, they left me alone. Aunt Melody did create a little windstorm of flower petals to surround me as I went outside to the patio. Being so connected to the elements, my aunts and father could manipulate the air around them to a certain extinct.

I felt better as I breathed the soft perfume from the flowers that still fell quietly around me. I loved my patio. When I moved into the house, the first thing I did was make this my sanctuary. I had watched one of those how-to shows on TV. It was only suppose to take a week but it took my mom and me three months. Of course most of my flowers are not real. My thumb is so far from green that plants should run if I approach. The few real plants that I have managed not to kill are spaced out here and there. The vines on the Pergola interweave unchecked through the ceiling beams for a nice wilderness effect. The bamboo trees lined the fence; they would grow everywhere if I was not careful. Since I could not lay the tile myself, Robert had helped clear part of my yard. Pavers were placed close together to form a stone foundation for my outdoor kitchen. The grass has overgrown them slightly which complements the area.

I had almost fallen asleep when some banging noises interrupted me. It came from the direction of Robert's house. I grabbed my footstool and padded my way through the bamboo stalks until I reached the fence. "Hi, there handsome. Come here often?"

"Keri-darling! What are you doing out so late?" He wiped his hands on his discarded shirt and walked over to the fence.

"I could ask the same thing. Who gardens in the dark? I just needed a little fresh air. What's all this?" I pointed to all the tubing and stakes on the ground.

"Well, I am installing and automatic feeding system for my garden. I'll be away for a few weeks and frankly, I can't trust you near my plants." His eyes twinkled a bit. I put my hands up in mock protest. He just looked at me. "I love ya, Keri-darling, but you could kill even those plastic contraptions over there in your yard."

I had to laugh. It was the truth. "Well my talents lay elsewhere. Anything you want me to do while you are gone?"

He stood up on a log and rested against the

fence. Grabbing his chin, he pondered my question. "Let's see...you can get my mail."

I saluted. "Check. Get mail."

"Hmm, drive my car a couple of times a week."

"Check. Have reckless abandonment in borrowed vehicle."

He motioned me closer. "And most importantly..." At that moment he kissed me. Not his normal cursory peck on the cheek but a deep, longing kissed filled with all the unspoken emotions he could not bring himself to say. "Don't go falling in love while I'm away."

The air changed from light and playful to thick and awkward. The kiss was nice but it did not move me. "Robert!"

He cupped my chin so I could not turn away from him. "I know you don't reciprocate my feelings." He looked over my shoulders towards the house. I could only imagine who his mind drifted to. But his eyes were soft when he said, "You have choices. You need to know that. You're my best friend. If that is all we ever will be, I still will still die a happy man."

I was shocked even though I knew how he felt. I

honestly thought he would never act on it. Maybe that was just wishful thinking on my part. "Robert, you know I care about you..."

"Don't say anything else. I am not asking how you feel. I just wanted you to know how I felt." He kissed my forehead and hopped down.

This day has definitely been one for the books. Sahaj. Panther. Robert. My nightmares would be a welcome diversion to reality at the moment.

Chapter 13 – I Lose My Temper…Again

Surely by now I must have brain damage. My head was throbbing from the viscous nightmare I had last night. I could not even think straight enough to write it down. I was heading to the shower when I noticed the faint aroma of coffee in the air. That made me quicken my pace. With four coffee lovers in the house at any given time I did not want it to run out. I popped some acetaminophen for my head and stepped in the shower.

The hot water was so refreshing that I could not rush through it. I stayed so long the hot water started to cool. I was hoping it would literally wash last night's bad dream away. It helped but not enough to remove the foreboding feeling that something bad was about to happen.

Slipping on a robe, I padded my way over to the sock drawer. My funky mood called for drastic measures. Out came my multicolored knee socks that had a slot for each toe from the drawer along with my favorite lime green boy cut underwear. I searched for my favorite navy tank top. Neo-soul was quickly found on my player. I needed something to dance to. I looked a bit frightful but it was my cheer-up outfit. Some people had comfort foods; I had comfort foods and clothes. This brought me to a serious need...butter pecan ice cream and coffee. Dancing my way downstairs, I headed for the fridge. I probably needed a proper breakfast but this was an emergency.

A hand flew around my waist and spun me around just as I had helped myself to a bit of ice-cream. Shocked I cried, "Pops, put me down." When I looked up though, I was not looking into Alexo's eyes. It was Sahaj's.

Stumbling back startled, "What are you doing here...*still?* Emphasis on the still."

He looked me up and down slowly – the I am checking you out and I want you to know it look. A smile crept across his face. "Currently, enjoying myself immensely."

That's when I realized I was only in my underwear. "Hold that thought. Actually don't. Excuse me." I flew back upstairs.

He yelled after me. "Don't change on my account...Please."

I was in the process of searching for some shorts when Alexo shimmered in. "Umm, was there something you needed to tell me?" He looked confused. I pointed downstairs. "Your little slumber party."

Now he looked sheepish. "Oh that. Well you know now. I knew animorphii existed but I had never met one. Time got away from me and I told him to crash in the guest room." He motioned for me to sit down. "We need to talk later. Robert agreed to research the symbols you were dreaming about. He will take them with him to India. I want to try to reach Teranodor."

I frowned up my face. "Let's try later. My head still hurts from last night."

He started rubbing my head. "The headaches are getting worst?" I nodded. "Your body is just getting use to your rapidly expanding mental capacity. I'm hoping they go away over time." His eyes flashed white briefly then smiled. "Come on. I think your aunts are having a little too much fun with Sahaj."

Back downstairs, my aunts were cooing over Sahaj who seemed to be putty in there hands as I walked in the room. "Ok ladies, you're going to spoil him." Aunt Melody shot me a knowing look.

Alexo sat on the counter in the kitchen while I made a fresh cup of coffee. My ice cream had since melted so I opted for some fruit to eat. As I ate my breakfast, images of Robert being tortured and beaten flew into my mind. It was a dark place lit only by candles. Men in masks circled around him. They held a knife to his throat. The knife bore one of the symbols from my dreams. The men chanted and slashed Robert's skin as if they were carving words into his body. Robert screamed out in pain and so did I. Angry, mad, scared I lashed out. Things started to fly around me bringing me back to reality. A knot formed in my stomach. My head became light and foggy then everything went black.

I did not know how long I was out for but judging from the look on everyone's face it must have been for some time. I just stayed on the cold tile floor and groaned. "Today is not going to be a good day.

Aunt Melody was leaning over me chanting, "*Sheave mi contra. Sheave vei.*" I could not understand what she said but just the sound of her voice was comforting. "Lay still little one." Her eyes flashed white and instantly Aunt Adiron was by my side with some cold juice.

Sugar always helped after I passed out. "What happened?" Sahaj looked flustered and relieved at the same time. He walked over and picked me up. He sat on the couch and nestled me in his arms. I tried to move but he would not let go of his death grip. I looked for Alexo but did not see him.

Aunt Adiron spoke quietly, "He had to return to Sirendll." She was anxious and a bit jumpy when she said that. Their faces said more than they did. Something had transpired while I was out. "Okay, which one of you is going to clue me in?"

Aunt Eiliel chimed in this time. "There was an accident." She paused to choose her words carefully. "Alexo was hurt in the process. He can heal faster in our realm."

"That's not telling me anything! What

happened? One moment I'm getting coffee and the next I'm on the floor." I was getting hot. The temperature in the room was rising in cadence with my emotions. Suddenly, the picture frames in the room exploded. Sahaj's grip tightened around me.

Aunt Adiron starting imitating the circular calming motion Alexo did. "Keridan you must calm down. Apparently your Siren abilities are growing but you are not in control of them yet. Your temper seems to trigger it." I exhaled trying to stay calm. "You looked as if you were having a vision when your kitchen started to fly about. Alexo moved to cover you but a knife went flying into his back. He was able to shimmer to Sirendll before the knife went too deep into his hearts. It still will take time to heal though."

This was awful. I was a menace. Understandably, I was new to the whole super power thing but this goes beyond the imaginable. Tears welled up in my eyes and began to flow uncontrollably down my cheeks. I almost killed my father. My life...this so called experiment...this human-Siren hybrid was a complete failure.

Sahaj pulled me onto his lap and I let myself be consoled. "Can I go to him?"

"We honestly do not know. We can try when you are up to it." Sahaj finally let me go. His shirt was soaked from all my sobbing. Aunt Melody wrapped her arms around me and shimmered. She left but I remained. Returning, she picked up a small statue that rested against the mantel. It disappeared with her. She came back and motioned for Sahaj. He stood. Grabbing his waist, she simmered again. I saw Sahaj disappear.

Deflated, I saw the prominent theme. "It's me. This is just wrong on so many levels."

Sahaj and Aunt Melody returned. He was a panther. I was not use to the panther in real life. He must have sensed my apprehension because he morphed quickly back into a man. "He is doing fine, Keridan."

"How is it that he gets to go? How could I be there when my mom died but not now?" I sounded more like a petulant child than a grown woman.

"First, He can only be there in his panther form. Secondly, you were not really in Sirendll before; it was just an illusion."

All this had made me forget why I was in this predicament in the first place. "Robert!" I got up and headed towards the door but was caught by

Sahaj.

"Where are you going? You need to rest."

I looked up at him then to the aunts. "Robert is in danger or he will be. He can't show the symbol. Oh it's all fuzzy now."

"What time was he leaving?"

I looked up at the clock. "Crap, he's already gone." I picked up my phone and searched for Robert's flight number. It was already in the air. "I'll have to wait at least seventeen hours." I started to pace knowing full well that it would not do me any good.

The aunts kept popping back and forth to check on Alexo now that I had calmed down some. Sahaj seemed to be waiting patiently for me. A host of emotions were going through my head. For one, I felt embarrassed that Sahaj had to see me like this. It was like he was intruding on my own little world of chaos. I could only imagine what he must think of me.

Looking to him, "I'm sorry about all this. I never dreamed to involve you in this drama."

He stood in front of me effectively halting my pacing. He pulled me into his arms and kissed me.

It was so soft and full of understanding. I was blown away. I was definitely going to have to set some ground rules with this man. "I have been alone for a long time. I have had secrets that I could not share with anyone. I understand what you are going through. If there is anything that I have learned over the course of my life is that when you find someone to share your life with it becomes better. I know we do not know each other well but I am officially in your life. It's going to take a lot to get rid of me." He cupped my chin. "Hey, I'm prince charming remember?"

I heard him, but something was nagging at me. "That's nice of you to say; just as long as we are clear that we are headed towards a friendship and nothing more."

"If that's what you want to call it. There is nothing friendly about how I feel for you. I, however, can wait until your heart catches up to mine." He traced his finger along my jaw sending tremors in it wake.

Being just his friend was going to be hard as my body was betraying my mind. With Alexo hurt and Robert in danger, getting to know Sahaj better was a low priority. He however made sure he was involved in everything for the rest of the day. I could admit to myself that I was ready to explore a deeper relationship with Sahaj. I was not sure if it was because of him or the fantasy I had created of him in my head over the past few weeks. I also knew that it would be better to wait. So many factors came into play. Was the attraction born out of this magical world that I was now a part of? Was it strong enough to overcome the hard parts? Was it just a matter of convenience? Was it just because I was lonely? I hoped my mind would figure it out before my heart was too far gone.

He kept my mood light by telling me about his past. He was an excellent story teller and I soon became engrossed in the tales of Puhave's sea-faring adventures.

"I have salt water in my veins." Sahaj said.

"I can't even swim. I'm not really a water person."

"Well, we'll have to do something about that."

"Right! Not going to happen. What does a former prince of the great naval empire of Puhave do everyday?"

"You mean besides babysitting damsels in

distress?" He pulled me closer to himself and sighed deeply. "You smell wonderful."

"Sahaj! You are not answering my question."

"Yes. Sorry, you have me a bit distracted." He buried his head into my hair and let out a little hissing sound. "That's the strangest part of my whole story. It seems the curse placed on me and Ida affected the survivors as well. The royal family was always taken care of by the populous. We were more of a trading society than anything. Although we did live in a palace it was very modest comparatively speaking. We were a community of small villages. My needs are still taken care of by the descendants of those few survivors. It appears to be hardwired in their DNA. When I am stuck in panther form, food is always readily available. As a man, money is always in my accounts to buy what I need."

"So let me get this straight. You don't have to work and money just magically appears."

"More or less. I am bound by the same laws as was established in Puhave – live simply, take care of your neighbors, things of that nature. I couldn't go out and buy a maserati. It isn't a need. The money just would not be there. I don't understand the *hows* or *whys* but I am grateful all the same."

"Interesting. So basically you are spoiled rotten. How do you get stuck in panther form?"

He tucked a stray piece of hair behind my ear. "If Ida hurts me in human form it triggers catastrophic events. Until, I heal or die the events continue. I can only heal in my panther state when she wounds me. When my country first sunk beneath the ocean, it was years before I could be fully human again. After I healed, the knowledge that I was responsible for so many deaths was more than I could bear. As a prince, I was brought up to respect life. The names and faces of my people still haunt me."

"But you can't possible believe that you were responsible. It's not like you cursed yourself."

"I am ultimately responsible for the safety of my people. I held no stock in the priests' determination to stop our union even after I turned into a panther. I saw what the priests were capable of and thought I was powerful enough to stop them."

"In hindsight, I was young and brash. I thought I could have the world. I was a prince and the people loved me. I was slightly arrogant but I have been humbled over the course of these past three hundred years. Did you know that male panthers are naturally loners? They are by themselves most of the time except when they cross a female. Even that is only a brief time period. As a panther, I am alone. As a human, I am hunted down and always on the run. Meeting you has truly been one of the best things that have happened to me."

He became silent, lost in his own memories. His pain mirrored my own. I drifted off to sleep for a much needed nap.

Chapter 14 – Where For Art Thou, Robert?

I woke headache free for the first time in what seemed like forever. My heart however was still heavy. I went first in search for my aunts then for my phone. I found both together downstairs in the kitchen.

Aunt Adiron was cooking something that smelled delicious. "Ah, she lives. Nice to have you back in the land of the living."

"Ha. Ha. What's this?" I dipped a spoon into the pot. It tasted like chicken soup.

"Are you feeling better?"

"Actually I feel great. I guess I just needed a good night's sleep."

Aunt Adiron held up three fingers. "What?"

"I'm correcting you. You feel great after three nights sleep."

"I've been asleep for three days!" She nodded. "Why did you let me sleep so long? Oh no! Robert!" I grabbed my phone.

"He called when he landed. I told him not to worry about the symbols until he talked to you." She held up her hand to silence further questions. "He was worried about you. He thinks you have a bad cold. You can try calling him after you go into the other room. Someone is waiting for you." She waved me off to finish her cooking.

I was shocked to see Alexo in the other room. He appeared to have aged a bit in the last few days. The one stark difference was the long silver dreadlock that fell to his shoulder. Light streamed through the window and bathed his face. It made his profile seem almost angelic.

I was actually nervous. What do you say to a man you almost killed? Even though it was an accident, I was still wary as I approached. He did not smile when he turned towards me which was so unlike him. I stood close to him not wanting to touch him just in case he was still in pain. I did not know much on Siren physiology. "Sorry." It was the only thing appropriate to say that I could think of.

He smiled at that. He picked me up and we did our little areal ballet. I felt wonderful, safe. I touched the silver strand when he put me down. "It's my battle scar. I'm okay. You can relax. I can feel your tension. What's a little life force among family right?"

"You are officially old now. You've aged an entire decade."

"Yes, well you have been changing a lot yourself. You feel up to some practice?"

"Sure." I owed him total cooperation after what I had put him through.

"Maybe we can get a good hour in before your panther shows up again."

"What!"

"Sahaj has barely left this house since you took ill. He is about to go crazy."

"Where is he now?"

"I sent him back to his place in hopes that *he* falls asleep for three days." He chuckled to himself. "So let's see if you can move things without nearly killing me." He put a pillow from the couch on to the coffee table. "Concentrate on the air around the pillow. Think about just moving the air."

I thought about hurricanes, windy days, and wind storms. Nothing. "I was angry every time I moved thing. Maybe I have to lose my temper."

"Let's hope not. Try again."

I concentrated, focused my entire mental capacity all to no avail. The pillow remained exactly where Alexo had put it. "The air is not moving. It must have been a fluke. I am just not wired like you are."

"That may be it. Your abilities seem to be slightly off from mine. Think about moving just the pillow. Leave the air alone."

I focused on moving the pillow. I really was at a lost on how to get it done. This was not exactly a skill taught in grade school. Nothing happened. "This is just frustrating. Why won't the thing just move?" While I slammed my fist down on my leg, the pillow shot across the room.

"Well that answers that. It too seems to be controlled by your emotions."

On the one hand, I was excited that my abilities were developing. On the other hand, how was a sometimes irrational, expressive train wreck, such as me, suppose to control my temper while balancing my other emotions? I had always been a bit of a hot head. There was just no way to turn that off.

While I was still frustrated, Alexo pushed me harder. It felt like basic training. We made connections until reality began to blur. Each time I landed on that beach Teranodor brought more Sirens. I was a postal worker who ferried messages across different dimensions.

My head throbbed. Even Alexo grew tired. So we took a break. I thought a quick walk would help. Alexo tagged alone. We talked about my Robert visions while we made our way through the neighborhood. It actually did clear my head. We even made it back to the house before dinner was done.

Aunt Adiron's latest culinary feast was spread out on the pedestals ready to be eaten. Mid-dinner Sahaj showed up. A rush of relief spread across his face. He crossed the short distance and lifted me off the ground in a big hug. He somehow fitted perfectly into my odd little family. That was a scary thought.

We were all resting, sitting around when Alexo's

eyes flashed a brilliant white. This was different than when he talked to my aunts. It repeated over and over. After it subsided, he came over to me. The aunts went suddenly to fuss over Sahaj. We walked into the kitchen for a little privacy. He held out his hand. I made a face. I did not think my mind could handle anymore connections today but I soon was back on my familiar beach. The scene had changed though. No Sirens were running about. One lone person trapped under a piece of driftwood. Running over, I pushed to log off of him. I was shocked to see it was Robert. His clothes were ripped. Sanskrit was written all over his body. He never opened his eyes. In the distance, a voice called my name. It came from all directions. The sky above began to actually rip apart like a painting being torn into pieces. Soon nothing was left. Four blank white walls with no windows or doors surrounded me.

The connection was broken. Blood trickled down the side of my forehead where a little scar was forming. Alexo's single silver dreadlock now had a mated pair. Both he and I were soaked in perspiration. I ran to get my phone and quickly dialed Robert's number. It was no longer in service. I was on the verge of hyperventilating. Alexo called to his sisters and Sahaj.

Out of the corner of my eye, I saw magazines, napkins, silverware start to shake. I yelled, "Stop!" One by one everything that was floating just dropped to the floor. Either time was slowing down or I was in a fog. Conversations were just an echo around me. After a few minutes, I could feel the cold countertop that I had been clutching. Normal time just snapped back like a stretched rubber band.

"I need to go to India to find Robert." I rummaged through the kitchen drawer to find his itinerary. "He should still be in Thiruvananthapuram. It may take me a while to get a flight. Could you shimmer there and start the search?"

"Yes, but I need to go to Sirendll first. Keridan, someone knows of you. I could feel someone in the connection. Adiron will stay here. Eiliel will stay in Sirendll. Melody will help me start the search."

Sahaj stepped around Aunt Melody. "I'm going with you."

"I appreciate the offer but..."

"No buts. I'm not letting you out of my sight. If someone wants to harm you then they'll have to go through me."

"Even better." Alexo joined in.

Apparently, I had my own personal hero. Alexo and my two aunts left us alone to make arrangements. I tried to book a flight but the earliest departure time was two days from now.

"Allow me." Sahaj held out his hand. "I need a plane to get to India in hopes to save a soul. Keys and a flight plan appeared in his hand. My mouth dropped. "A prince's need shall be fulfilled as long as the need and the cause are real."

Aunt Adiron started to clap. "Oooh, Keridan, can we keep him? Can we?"

Chapter 15 – Plane Rides Make Me Nervous

We headed over to the airfield where a private plane was waiting for us. A nice Indian pilot bowed slightly to Sahaj and spoke quietly in a different language. Sahaj left with the pilot after they showed me to a couch.

The interior of the plane was very plush. There was a TV screen off to my left with a compartment by the chair that contained DVD's. Headphones hung from a hook below the built-in player.

This would be a frightening experience for me. I did not do well in the air. After all the strange things that have happened to me of late, I should be stronger; but my stomach was in knots.

Sahaj came up beside me. "We should be leaving soon. Let's get settled in." After sitting back down, I buckled myself in. The flight attendant came over and gave us the normal pre-flight spill then disappeared behind a curtain. "You look blue."

"It'll pass. I am no good on planes."

He moved closer to me, draped his arm on the back of my seat. He leaned over and kissed me. He nibbled on my bottom lip followed by soft butterfly kisses up my jaw line. My shoulders, cheeks and eyes all fell prey to his expert salutations. Frustration and tension melted away from my mind. Minutes flew by like seconds as I started down the path to losing all sense of reason. "See that was not so bad."

It was then I realized we were already up in the air. "Smug male."

He continued basking in his maleness. "We have a few hours to kill. What do you want to do first plan, nap or watch movies?"

"Definitely plan. I have never been out of the States before."

"Don't worry. This is my old stomping ground."

I settled into the sofa and grabbed a blanket to get comfortable. "Tell me about that. You said your people had fled to India." He took the blanket from me pulling me into his arms. He was warm, really warm. I had never noticed that before.

He rubbed my arms trying to warm me up. "Years ago my great grandfather was approached by the Raja of the Cholas dynasty. He was amazed by our ship building techniques. He wanted to make an alliance with Puhave. Our two countries shared culturally for a few years then we started trade routes from Tamil Nadu to Malaysia. Our massive ships could hold up to four hundred people at a time. When the tsunami hit we had only three big ships that weren't destroyed. As many people as we could find were loaded into those ships. We set sail to our closest alliance which was Sri Lanka. Even after hundreds of years and the fall of the Cholas we still maintained good relations with the people of South India. Most of the Royal Family left for Kanyakumari. There was at that time great expansive jungles that stretched up the coast of Tamil Nadu and Kerala where I could roam as a panther and still be close to my family.

"I thought you did not have to stay a panther."

"No, I only have to be a panther to heal. If I am wounded though and the world around me is thrown into chaos then the longer I stay in panther form the quicker the pain of the world subsides."

I settled in a bit more. "You have experienced so much loneliness. It hurts me. I wish I could help erase the bad parts."

He looked so deep into my eyes, I felt him peering straight into me. "You have done much more than you know."

I thought we were talking about two different things but I let it go. As I went to grab my bag, he began rubbing my back. Little lightening bolts dotted my skin in places where he touched. He started kissing the back of my neck which made alarms go off in my head. Kissing my neck was definitely going down a path that led to trouble. I started to stand but his hand caught my waist. He let out a hiss.

"Did you just hiss at me?"

"You keep wiggling."

"Well, you keep going over the boundaries."

"Boundaries? Is this a boundary?" He kissed my wrist. I shook my head no. He kissed my forehead. "How about here?" I shook my head no. "Here." He moved my hair and planted a kiss at the base of my neck.

"Out of bounds!"

He inhaled deeply. "Interesting." He rubbed the spot he just kissed with his thumb.

"Look we need to make a plan on how to find Robert."

"Robert. Right. You need to stop distracting me."

"I am not doing anything to you."

"Oh but you are. You scent is driving me insane. You wake up the animal in me, literally."

"Sahaj!"

"Okay. Focus. Robert. I get it." He put on his most angelic face.

I was not convinced but he maintained somewhat good behavior while we went through Robert's itinerary. He was scheduled to meet with a professor friend of his from the University of Kerala in Thiruvananthapuram. Dr. Kanari was setting up meetings for him with members from some of the Schedule Tribes of India located in Kerala and Tamil Nadu. I would need to contact him first to see when the last time he had seen Robert.

Dr. Kanari apparently was a famous

archaeologist. He was currently doing a dig not far from Kanyakumari, in between teaching at the university. Robert had dog-eared some articles published about Dr. Kanari. They were included in a stack of papers he had left at his house which I had quickly ransacked before we left searching for anything that would help me find him. He kept everything. He was a paper pack rat. Sticky notes and empty envelopes were his paper of choice. I grabbed everything I could fit into a backpack.

I had to chuckle at all the cryptic papers in front of me. Robert wrote exactly like he talked – fast and excitedly. When he tried to convey a thought too quickly you could barely understand his scribble scratch. I did come across a couple of sticky notes that just said, "Keri-darling." I was going out on a limb to say that traipsing across the world to save Robert would do more harm than good in squelching his love feelings for me. I would have to tamp those feeling down when I returned, if I returned. He would do the same for me. He has done the same for me in some regards. In fact, he has been there for me so many times that it would be ridiculous for me not even to try especially when I am probably the cause of his pain anyway. That guilt would live with me forever even if he turned out to be okay.

Sahaj gave me a crash course on Indian culture. He taught me a few phrases in Tamil in case we got separated. I found out that he had not been to India since it gained its independence from the British. Talking to him was like watching the history channel which happened to be one of my favorite past times. The more I listened to him, the easier it became to detect his accent. It was faint, subtle and soothing.

I must have fallen asleep somewhere after one of his jungle adventures. It was now dark outside. Sahaj was sprawled over the sofa that lined the opposite wall. Serving trays lay on the table. Seeing them made me realize how hungry I had become. I began to wonder if I could control my telekinetic powers. My anger controlled so much of my new found abilities. I needed to find a stronger emotion to overpower it. I looked over at Sahaj and felt a peaceful calm pour over me. I thought about that tray and tried to get it to move hoping that the plane would not move with it. I did notice it moved a few inches. Maybe there was hope for me yet. Alexo would have been proud. My thoughts made it back to Robert. My best friend was in danger. Oddly, I was more worried about him then about whoever was after me. This could all be a wild goose chase. Robert could be sitting in his hotel room watching TV. He was known for losing his phone.

I was grasping at straws but it was the only way to hope. I knew my connections were real to some extinct, what I did not know was how Robert came to be in them.

Chapter 16 – New Places, New Faces

The plane landed early morning the next day. I was surrounded by the bright beautifully rich colors. Sari-clad women were selling flowers they had just weaved. It reminded me of the leis from Hawaii. I bought some to wear. There was a car waiting for us at the airport.

The driver bowed to Sahaj and spoke softly in Tamil. Sahaj looked a little perturbed briefly but spoke very gently back to the driver. He grabbed the bags then held the door open for me. I could tell Sahaj's mood had changed. Maybe he was jetlagged.

The ride was harrowing. The driver weaved in and out of traffic. The streets were filled with vendors selling their wares on both sides. In fact, at these speeds it looked like there were not even any spaces between the makeshift stores. Auto rickshaws, bikes and motorcycles all competed with cars for road space.

We arrived at the hotel and I noticed the stickiness in the air. The hotel though made up for the overcast sky and mugginess from the outside. Gold silk and plush red velvet lined the windows. We had a suite with two bedrooms. Everything was clean and the people were helpful. We settled in. I thumbed through some magazines however Sahaj's mood did not improve.

"Is there something wrong?"

"Not yet. It is just this place. I forgot how closely connected to it I was."

"What do you mean? Is this about the driver? You seem to be in a funky mood ever since we met him. I'm sure we can find another way around."

"It's not him. He will be our driver for the remainder of the trip. Hanupreesh, that's his name. He is a descendant of a Puhave survivor. One drawback to the curse is how the people are hardwired to serve me. They don't even know why. Being in the States for so long, made me forget how it felt. Over there if I needed something it just appears. Over here it appears with people attached. It makes being a man that much harder."

"Are you worried about Princess Ida finding you?"

"That's a real danger being over here for too long. Magic leaves traces. There are more descendants over here which means more traces, but it is more than that. I could not live with myself if I brought harm to you...if you somehow ended up wounded by my past."

"Hey, I'm a big girl. I can take care of myself. Everything will work out."

Sahaj started to say something when Alexo shimmered into the room. The first thing I noticed was another silver dreadlock had appeared on his head. Alexo looked at Sahaj for a long moment. He then bowed his head slightly and squeezed my shoulders.

I hugged Alexo. "Hi Pops! What happened?" I fingered the silver strand.

He kissed my forehead quickly, "That's not important right now. We have a problem."

I opened the newspaper he handed me. "Local

professor murdered at archeological site...The body of Dr. Kanari, professor of history was brutally stabbed yesterday..." I finished reading the article. Shock was still over my face.

"The good news is when I spoke with him yesterday he had already met with Robert. Dr. Kanari had set Robert up with a guide down in Kanyakumari and one in the Wayanad district. He was to go to Kanyakumari first. The bad news is that I found no trace of him ever making it. His hotel had him checked out here in Thiruvananthapuram. He never checked in Kanyakumari. Have you had any flashes?"

I thought about that. My head has been so full of other things. "No. Not a flash or a dream actually." I fervently tried to remember as much as I could. I pulled out a copy of the writing I had seen on Robert's body. "Can we narrow down anything from these writings?"

Sahaj picked up the sketches I had drawn on the plane. His eyes went wide. "When did you do these? Keridan, this is written to you." Alexo rushed over. He read the writings.

"As I am not fluent in anything but French, could one of you clue me in?"

Sahaj looked at me. "French?" I gave him a perturbed look. "Okay." He threw his hands up. "It basically says you can travel to lands end to find your loved ones and friends but it will be too late for the world. You must choose."

"Okay, that is a little unnerving. What have I done to anyone?"

Alexo came over, grabbed my hand and led me to the couch. "A few years back there was a Siren, Nefer, who did not totally prescribe to our peace efforts. He felt the need for power and domination. The council stripped him of all his abilities and banished him to a human life in the mortal realm. Teranodor was assigned to watch over him. The council wiped his mind of Sirendll...of anything connected to Sirens. I believe something has happened. It all fits. When we lost Teranodor we sent people out to find him. Do you remember him speaking of the "searchers"? He must have traced you through the other Sirens, through their connections. What we know is that the missing Sirens can not communicate telepathetically or shimmer, as you call it?"

"But why Robert? Why me for that matter?"

"Well you were able to get through whatever he

had used to block the others. Your abilities would make him more invincible."

Sahaj turned into a panther and let out a hissing sound. He crouched down protectively in front of me. "I am not sure how Robert plays into all of this other than using him to get to you. Maybe the original symbol has something to do with it after all."

"I found similar markings on the site where Dr. Kanari was murdered." Aunt Melody opened her palm to show a small rock that was carved.

"So let's assume that Robert did show Dr. Kanari the symbol. Where do we now start looking? Is there another way to find out what the symbol means?" I had a thought. "Sahaj, how many Indian dialects do you know?"

He morphed into a man. I just noticed that he had the same clothes back on. "Not nearly all of them."

"Can you tell if this is from a language? Robert thought it may be Dravidian in origin."

"It does not appear to be some form of Sanskrit. The lines are slightly off."

"Pops, I think we need to go to the Wayanad District." I walked over and picked up a map from my bag. "See, here, Robert was going to Kanyakumari and Kalkishin. The site where Dr. Kanari was found was not directly on the way to the Wayanad District. The message said land's end but I feel that is not the first place we need to look." I kept reading over the notes Robert left, but there was nothing in it that gave me a clue.

I started thumbing through the brochures left on the table again deep in thought. There were pages and pages of advertised tours to take. One in particular caught my attention. "Pops, these caves have similar markings carved on them. It says they are ancient petro glyphs made by a civilization that lived here six thousand years ago - even before *your* time." I could not help myself on that note.

He smiled a little. Aunt Melody brought over the rock while Alexo held up the magazine. He agreed they were pretty close. "We can start there. Get some rest. It will take several hours for you to get there by car. Melody and I will go ahead and start looking for any signs of Robert. The area is mostly jungle so you need to get some gear. You can leave at first light."

"Do you have a cell phone, now? How do I contact you? I can't do the flashy eye trick." He came and gave me a big hug.

"Are you missing me already?" He laughed. "Let's see if you can wind whisper. Your other powers are developing. Close your eyes, picture me in you mind, then whisper *Savoy Chauncii.* That opens an air channel connection to me. It's like the connections we make with our palm but not as strong. I will not be able to get into your head but I will be able to know your location. Try it."

He went into the other room. I spoke the words. The air crackled like static from the radio. Alexo shimmered in and swung me around. "So you heard me in your head?" I asked.

"Loud and clear."

"Are you sure it was not just your supersonic hearing?"

He seemed to sober up a little. "What is this all about?"

I pointed to the new silver strand on his head. "Just worried I guess."

He kissed my hand. "Be strong little one. It will all work out in the end."

What was that? I looked over to Sahaj who seemed very preoccupied at the moment. I turned back just in time to hear a soft goodbye float through the air as Alexo and Aunt Melody shimmered away. He never did answer the question.

Chapter 17 – Bedtime Stories

"So, do you want to nap or would you like to look around a bit?"

"Let's go shopping. Apparently, I need some jungle gear. I have a sinking feeling that I will be going off the tourist path."

Hanupreesh was waiting for us outside. He took us to the Chalai Market. It was a wonderfully busy place. My first thought as we walked through the market was about teal paint. As an artist I seldom ever used teal paint. It was too strong for most things, but this market was the land of the lost teal. From crates to walls to roofs, teal was everywhere.

The bright colors complemented the fruits and

vegetables being sold off the street. Bananas of every size hung down from tin roofs. Fish lay cut open over ice barrels which were sold next to electronics. This market was a mish mash cornucopia of everything you could possibly need.

People were crushed all around me in the streets. I wondered into one of the cafes to break from the throng. It sold pastries and Indian coffee. Being a self proclaimed coffee connoisseur, I had to try some. It was spicy and sweet reminiscent of a pumpkin latte.

Back in the midst of the crowd, we loaded up on cherries, grapes and mangoes. After that, Hanupreesh took us to get some outdoor basics – first aid kits, sunscreen, and small foldable tents. I was no where near a camping person but would rather be over prepared than under prepared.

The plan was to travel to Kalkishin and check out the caves. There would be an Adivasi guide to lead us into the part of the jungle where some more petro glyphs were located. These were not in the tour books.

After what seemed like hours, we headed back to the hotel where Sahaj ordered us dinner. I decided to take a shower before the food showed up. It felt strange to be here, half a world away from every thing I knew. My life had drastically changed over the last few months, but this appeared to be just the beginning of my journey. I felt strong just being here. Up until this point, I went through my days being sheltered from life itself. I worked my jobs and felt I was good at it. I balanced my business side with my creative side. My perspective of what was important or what was considered dangerous shifted to encompass the possibility of magic and myth.

My emotions were still a little raw when I slipped on my robe. Wonderful smells drifted my way so I assumed the food had arrived. Sahaj must have showered because he was now dressed in a loose white cotton shirt and pants. He was lounging on the couch.

The table was set with candles. Little pastries, cut-up fruits and sliced vegetables were arranged on colored plates. Two covered dishes were in the center of the little table. Sahaj's eyes followed me as I moved around the room. It did not make me nervous but definitely more self-aware and self-conscious.

"Come show me what's good. I have never had Indian food before."

He walked over to me. "Well, traditional Indian

meals always start with dessert." With that he kissed me lightly on the lips. I swatted at him while he just chuckled. "No, seriously, this is Aloo Gobi. It is cauliflower, potatoes and tomatoes stewed in a curry sauce." He uncovered the next dish. "This is buttered chicken. This is chocolate burfi. It's like a brownie."

He made me a plate then made himself one. The food was really good even the curry dish and I was not a big fan of curry. After eating we went to lounge on the couch. I was tired even though it was still relatively early.

"You smell wonderful."

Sahaj grabbed his chest as if he was having a heart attack. "What is this…a compliment…from Keridan? Impossible!"

"What is that suppose to mean?"

"You are a hard woman, Keridan. Although I know you like me, I'm not sure you have figured that out yet."

"You read too much into things. I was just stating a simple fact."

"See, hard woman."

The food had put me in a happy place. I

snuggled closer into him. His arm automatically pulled me into his lap. I played with the smooth hair on his arms. I think my heart was winning this round. I liked the peaceful feeling I had when I was with him. Circled in his arms, I felt safe and protected. I turned to look him in the eyes. Suddenly, I felt the urge to kiss him. His eyes grew large, startled, as I pressed my lips to his. A passion–filled volcano erupted in me. I straddled his lap to get better access to his lips, his chest and neck. His hands slid inside my rode, palming the small of my back while simultaneously pulling me closer to him. We melted into one massive body.

After what felt like forever, I had to come up for air. Sahaj's eyes were still filled with heat. My heart continued to race and my body screamed for completion. Sahaj placed kisses on the top of my breast right above the neckline of my pajamas. I arched my back and his mouth captured my budding breasts totally soaking my camisole top. He blew on them making the hardened pearls grow even more. Little shimmers went down my spine.

My mind started to win over my treacherous body. I did not want to be pegged a tease but I had to find a way to stop before we went too far. I had just started to work out my feelings for him. I did not need to add more complications. I started this escapade now I needed to will myself to stop.

I curled back into his chest waiting for my heart rate to return to normal. Eventually our breathing matched each other in a slow song. I stole a peek up at him. His wide smile told me more than his smoldering eyes did.

"I'm not hard all the time."

"I stand corrected. Please feel free to correct me anytime."

"I might just do that."

"Does this mean that you are ready for me to be a more permanent fixture?"

"Maybe."

"You still have reservations?"

"Oh, loads of them. Time will sort them out."

"Well, time I have. How about you get some sleep?"

"I'm tired but not sleepy."

Chuckling, "I bet. Would you like a bed time story?"

"This ought to be good."

"Quiet."

I settled in still laying on his chest. "Many years ago, there was a hot, steamy jungle in a land that had no name. The land had no name because it lacked the people to name it. Though no people were there, the land was home to many animals. There were the monkeys who were tricksters and slithering snakes that saw all. There were birds of all shapes, colors and sizes."

"But from the beautiful butterfly to the biggest bear, none was greater than the black panther. All animals lived in harmony and through the land there was peace. One day, the monkey said to the black panther, *'there's a new fish in the water.'* Well, the panther knew the monkey liked to play games so he did not believe him. However, the panther walked down to the beach to see for himself. Indeed, a great fish made of trees was sitting in the water."

"Curious, the panther waited to see if the fish would get any closer. The monkey went to gather up the other animals so they too could watch the big fish. The big fish came to shore but it was not a fish at all. It was just a container that carried other animals. The hairless animals walked out of the tree container."

"Now there was a female that disembarked and

walked onto the beach. Her beauty was so great that it silenced all the animals. The panther was so struck that he left his brush cover and walked towards the beautiful one. She knelt beside him and stroked his fur. She turned to the other hairless animals still in the container and they moved the container back to the water. She picked up some sand and whispered Puhave. At once the panther turned in a male hairless animal. He ruled over all animals in the land. He called the land Puhave after the words that spoke him free."

I could not manage to say anything as I was almost asleep. Vaguely, I felt him picking me up and taking me to my room.

Chapter 18 – The Depth Of Love

Walking through a dark cavern, I breathed the thick, aged air. I was intruding on centuries of isolation. Stalactites and stalagmites dotted the corridor. Those menacing rock formations coupled with the slick surfaces caused by a constant drip of water made it difficult to maneuver around. A low hum from up ahead could be barely heard above the shuffling of my feet. The tunnel started to shake. Twenty feet in front of me rocks fell from the ceiling allowing for a waterfall to push through. The fallen rocks did not just fall down. They formed an altar. A perfectly healthy Robert materialized in the room. He did not even notice me. He stared down at the alter watching a different body appear on the new altar.

I woke feeling weird. This was not one of my

normal nightmares. It was not exactly a nightmare at all. I looked at the clock. It was four in the morning. We were going to get an early start but this was a bit too early. I was thinking too coherently to go back to sleep so I decided to get on up. Beginning to pack, I became distracted by sounds outside the window. There was some commotion below. Briefly, I saw some men dressed in all black. "Well, I guess I am not the only one who cannot sleep."

Oddly, the men in black appeared to look in my direction. I was three stories up. My favorite panther came barging in the room and planted his immense lean body against the window sill. It would look a little strange even through the shadows of the curtain to see Sahaj morph from panther to man so I turned the lamp off but was still startled. The men still looking up were soon diverted by the scene in front of them.

"Not that I mind you being here, but could you clue me in to what's going on?" He morphed into a man.

"You need to pack quickly. No Lights. Please stay away from the window. There is someone down there who is trying to find you. Someone not totally human I would wager. I was lounging with the window open. People below started preparing for the festival early and it woke me. Those men in black were looking for the Siren girl. Then you started talking to yourself and they honed in on you."

He went to the window to peek down. "They have moved away. Keep the light out just in case they are just out of view."

"How did you hear them? Or me for that matter?"

"I sleep as a panther. My senses are more aware."

"Do you always sleep as a panther?"

He stood very close to me and looked hard into my eyes. "Unless, I have a reason not to do so." He briefly brushed his knuckles across the base of my throat.

"And in three hundred or so years, how many times have you had a reason not too?" I started to fidget and my mind was mentally wandering to forbidden territories. He cocked his head a bit. "Don't answer that – at least for now. Bad guys running rampart. I am focused."

He picked me up, nestled me in the crook of his

elbow and kissed me. "I like that you are curious, maybe even a little jealous and a whole lot more receptive." He put me back down and walked out of my room.

What was that! I thought to myself.

Before we left I thought I had better contact Alexo. I did the wind whisper thing and waited for him to appear. He showed up not much later. It made me giddy each time I did something out of the normal, well under my former definition of normal. I guess the newness has not worn off yet.

"Yes little one." He hugged and spun me around.

"Did I wake you?"

"No, we really do not have to sleep. We just rest from time to time."

I processed that for a moment. "Oh we'll talk about that later. There was a man here for me earlier. Sahaj wanted to quickly get on the road."

He was a little alarmed. "I had not realized it would be this soon." Sahaj came into the common area. "Listen. I can not trace you unless you use your abilities. Your human side blocks that. I can not get into your head either. I feel your best defense, at least until we know more about what Nefer is up to, is to limit using them. So do not go making people fall in love with you." He looked to Sahaj. "Well at least anyone else. No telekinesis. No call. Just be as completely human as you can muster."

"How can you want me to be defenseless?"

"You will not be defenseless. You have me." Sahaj interjected. "I will protect you with my life."

As comforting as that was, I still felt vulnerable. I tried to put on my brave face and shake off my nerves. "How are things coming along with the search?"

"We have been combing the caves and have found no traces of Robert. The hotel did remember him being there though."

"Were any of the caves underground?"

"No why?"

"I just dreamed of an underground cave last night. Most of my dreams of late have meant something." I explained everything I could remember to Alexo and Sahaj. We went over the details of where to meet. I was told to look touristy and blend in.

Nefer was looking for a female Siren so he needed to track a magical trail. Alexo shimmered away back to the caves. Shortly after he left my palm started to itch. Then a searing pain shot through the deep brown life lines on my hand. I watched as orange light seeped from the creases. Tears welled up in my eyes and I fell to my knees in pain. Sahaj rushed to my side. I balled up hoping the pain would not last much longer.

The pain started to ease but was replaced by a huge scar covering my entire palm. I sucked in my breath and motioned for Sahaj. We needed to hurry it was almost sunrise. With tears still welling up in my eyes, I tasted blood from where I bit my lip trying not to scream.

We slowly made it downstairs. Hanupreesh was waiting for us. I searched the street for our guests but they were empty now. Sahaj held my good hand while we sat in the back of the car. He lightly touched the space around the scar careful not to touch the blistered parts. His eyes questioned what was going on with me. I could tell. "I do not know what it means. It just hurts." Although it had shrunk a little since we left the hotel room the pain had not decreased any more.

"You make me feel helpless when you cry." He used the back of his hand to wipe an escaped tear from my cheek. "What can I do?"

"Nothing." I glanced over at the back of Hanupreesh's head. "If I know anything about my new alternative lifestyle is not to be surprised when unusual things happen to me."

Time passed rather slowly. Sahaj talked about some of the landmarks of the Wayanad district on the way. He told me of the chain tree where an Adivasi, native tribal Indian, guided a British engineer through this area of India. The engineer wanted the credit for discovering this particular part of the country so he killed the guide. The Adivasi's spirit was understandably angry so he began to attack the travelers that came this way. There was a priest who captured the troubled spirit and chained it to the tree. With all that has happened to me, I could now believe that an actual spirit was magically pinned down there.

We continued up the coast of Kerala all morning. Hanupreesh wove in and out of traffic. Multicolored buildings came in and out of view. It reminded me more of downtown Atlanta; more so of how Atlanta looked twenty years ago before the renovations.

Parts of the highway gave way to beautiful beaches where you could just pull over and walk to the ocean. I would love to be able to explore this place when I could actually enjoy it.

About five hours into our journey we stopped in Calcutta to get some food. The pain in my hand had lessened considerably but the scar remained. We did not linger, just staying long enough to stretch and eat. By mid-afternoon we were at the hotel.

Hanupreesh and Sahaj spoke quietly while I waited by the bags. We headed upstairs to the room. This hotel was not as nice as the one we stayed before but it was clean. It was only a one room suite. I was getting around to asking about sleeping arrangements when Aunt Melody shimmered in. Relief washed over her face.

"Little one, I am glad you have made it safely. I thought something was wrong." She hugged both me and Sahaj. "When your father left this morning, he seemed slightly on edge."

"Didn't he tell you what happened?"

"No. He has not been back since he left. I remained in the caves while he went to check on you. I assumed he was with you."

"No. He left before we did."

Her eyes went white in a blaze of bright light and did not return to normal until several minutes later. "Adiron or Eiliel have not seen him either."

I tried to wind whisper to him but received no response. Aunt Melody looked worried. I went over to her and rubbed her back the way Alexo did. I knew it did not work the same but it was all I could think of. The scar started to itch. Absentmindedly, I scratched it. I would need to find some salve to put on it pretty soon. I wondered if normal medicine would work on magical wounds…probably not.

"What's wrong little one?" She took my hand. I explained the pain from this morning and how the scar appeared. Tears welled up in her eyes.

"Stupid, stupid man!" She plopped down on the bed. Plopped did not describe it accurately. She floated gracefully in the air for a while and sort of landed on the bed. I looked down at my hand then over to Sahaj. Maybe she read my palm and it was not good.

Her eyes looked lifeless when she looked up. She motioned for me to come over. Taking my hand she lightly traced the scar. "Alexo has marked you." Seeing my confusion she went on to explain. "Sirens make connections not only to communicate but also to form bonds - to mate. If the male initiates the bond it is permanent. If the female initiates the bond the permanence is only set when consummated."

Looking down at my hand, I flipped it over. "What are you talking about? Are you saying my father wanted me to be his wife? That sounds creepy on so many levels."

"No Keridan. How can I elucidate? Your father never mated – never took a wife, as you called it. You have been his entire world since the day you were conceived. Your father has chosen to not ever take one. He has basically said his life is complete; but, in doing so, he has also set the time of his death. Obviously you cannot complete the connection. He knew that. If you choose to make a mated connection in the future to a Siren he dies." This must have interested Sahaj because he came to sit down on the bed beside me.

"Okay, no worries. I won't ever mate with a Siren."

"Little one, it is more complicated than that. He did more that just take your choice away." She glanced over to Sahaj. "Connections are complex. To be mated with a Siren means to share abilities, to share thoughts. I am not just talking about regular telepathy. You experience life as a mated being. What happens to one is shared by the other. If you were fully Siren as soon as Alexo made the connection you would have access to his thoughts, his entire mind until the day he passed on. You would be able to channel his ability to fly. These shared abilities come at a price if not balanced properly. If abused by either party then the life force gets drained."

"That puts me right back at my previous statement. If I never mate with a Siren – the entire world is right again."

"Yes, little one that is essentially correct; however although Alexo did was what he thought to be a show of ultimate love for you left you vulnerable. I am sure he was trying to show you how much you meant to him, to make up for the twenty-five years that he did not get to be a part of your life. Keridan, please understand that not all mated connections are made by choice."

I started to feel the sickness beginning to wash over me. I willed myself to not pass out. "You are trying to tell me that if I do not willingly choose a Siren, I may be made to unwillingly choose one.

Nefer."

"Yes. Do not you see? You are more powerful than you realize. You are a matched set. You have Siren abilities as well as some unique human qualities. We know he can control the Sirens somehow. He knows that you can get past whatever magical resources he is using. He needs you. He wants your power to add to his collection. It is not just Nefer though. Has your father not told you who he was?"

"What? He told me he was a prince? I know he is a peace keeper. We never really dove deeper than that. He was pushing me too hard for anything else."

"Little one, your father is a bit more than that. He is the highest above all the elemental ruling families even higher than the Council of Sirens. He is the power behind that ruling body. It is not well known how powerful he actually is just for safety reasons. We are a peaceful people but your father has many enemies known and unknown. The knowledge of this connection could destroy both him and you."

"I would never even under duress though side with Nefer or anyone else. I like to think I am capable of making my own choices."

"Really, not even to save Alexo or Robert?"

"But if what you say is true, then a connection between Nefer and me would kill Alexo."

"He does not know. We did not even know. Only a Siren has the ability to read each other's thoughts. Nefer has shown that he still does not have his abilities. His memories have just come back."

"Wait a minute! You said that I would be able to share abilities, thoughts, but Alexo could never get into my head. What about my ability to move things."

"I now believe that your human side filters his ability to move the air around things allowing for you to actually move objects rather than just the air. We, your aunts and I, just assumed he had been up to no good when his life force began to deplete. We had no idea."

"His hair…the silver tendrils, that's how you knew, right?" She nodded.

"Nefer does not understand what makes you so different. He would never dream that some of your talents are so intrinsically linked to Alexo. If he did he would not have taken him. Your very existence is inimitable. The program was discontinued after your mother almost lost her life trying to deliver you. Sadly, he is so disturbed that I do not see him ever stopping until he has you."

"How are you so certain that it is Nefer that has Alexo? What if he is just somewhere hurt and can't shimmer?"

She turned over her palm. She had the same faint scar as me. My eyes widen in the realization, "Teranodor."

Chapter 19 – I Met Myself

This whole time Sahaj had just been listening, albeit attentively, but soon he came to life. "She's not safe here. Alexo said she needed to not do magic; but she will not be able to help herself if she is attacked. They found her in Thiruvananthapuram."

"What do you propose?"

"I'll take her to the jungle."

"How is that going to help? We need to find away to get her out of here – out of India. Now that we know a little more about Nefer, the council can come in and help clean this up."

"Forgive me but the council did not do such a good job the first time. If he has found a way to neutralize Sirens, what good would an army of Sirens do?"

"No, forgive me, but what good would having her sit under a banana tree do?"

I threw up my hands. "Enough! I know both of you are trying to do what is best for me but, frankly, I will be the judge of what is good for me. I am not going to abandon Robert or Alexo or Teranodor. Not when we are close. What is a little life force among loved ones? Is there another way into Sirendll besides shimmering?"

"No."

"Okay, Aunt Melody, then you are officially grounded. Aunt Eiliel will need to coordinate with the council. We started this adventure because of Robert. Our focus needs to remain there. This is bigger than just my safety. I need you two to understand that. Sahaj and I will work on the connection between the symbol, Robert and Nefer. See if you and Aunt Adiron can work on a location for Nefer."

"He can be anywhere little one."

"No, he is here is in India. The message on Roberts's body stated *land's end*. That is Kanyakumari. We just need to find out what both the Wayanad district and Kanyakumari have in common." I handed her my cell phone. "Take this to contact me. I can't hear you on the wind whisper thing; and I do *not* want you to shimmer anywhere. Sahaj's number is programmed."

My bravado was beginning to get a little shaky. I needed a little air before I broke down on both of them. I took one of the maps out of my bag and went over to the window pretending to need more light. They seemed to accept that I needed a moment because they left me alone. It was hard to grasp the severity of the situation at the tail of the confrontation. How was I to stop a crazed Siren, rescue Alexo and Robert all while not becoming a victim myself? I have been so wrapped up in myself that it never dawned on me to try to fully understand the complexities of being Siren. Looking back, I can vaguely recall snippets of conversations. I barely remembered the deliberate looks Alexo would give me in attempt to get me up to speed. I wasted so much time.

I started to repack my backpack for things I needed in the jungle. Sahaj moved quietly to my side. It was time to go. Hugging Aunt Melody, a few small tears grudgingly slipped down my cheek. I hoped that what ever was coming would come soon.

I expected to see Hanupreesh when we made it

downstairs; however, instead, Sahaj went over to the front desk and was given two back packs. We walked outside and he began to open the bags. Inside each bag was a folded bicycle. My eyes grew wide.

"We will be off road, so these will be our mode of transportation. Can you handle it? It is about 20 kilometers to where we are going."

"Uhh – do you remember when I told you I was not an outdoor person? I *really* was not joking."

"Keridan, it's either riding the bikes or riding a big black panther." He flashed me a smile which led me to believe he was holding out for the latter. "The bike does most of the work. It is motorized." He patted my shoulders and gave me a slight push towards the bike.

I strapped my back pack tighter to me and adjusted my helmet. It had been so long since I rode a bike. I was having flash backs to my little pink and purple two wheeler with the tinkling bell on the handlebars and glittery streamers. I pulled out onto the road and kept close to Sahaj. I thought it would be disorienting to be on the wrong side but I became use to it. I had been driven everywhere so I never noticed.

Thirty minutes later we veered off the main road. It was not exactly a road we were traveling on more of a well trodden path. Above our heads the canopy of the jungle grew thicker as we moved forward. Thick vines and oversized leaves blocked most of the sky letting only sparse streams of sunlight escape to the ground.

As we continued deeper into the jungle, we came across a small patch of water that had a fallen tree across it which we had to traverse. I remember reading about how coconut tree trunks were used to make small bridges. It was tricky to balance myself and the bike but I slowly made it across.

Sahaj slowed as we approached a grove of thickly knarled trees. He hopped off the bike, folded it up and put it in the bag. "Welcome home." I looked to the top of the trees. There was a tree house nestled between several forked branches.

"I hope there is an elevator because my tree climbing days have passed."

Sahaj folded down my bike and put it in the bag. He morphed into a panther, put the handle of both bags in his mouth then climbed the tree closest to us. He seemed to bounce gracefully from limb to limb with ease. He looked like an overgrown kitten playing on one of those carpeted cat climbers.

"Hey, Bagheera, if you have not noticed I am not exactly Mowgli." He hissed at me, but shortly afterwards a rope ladder rolled down the tree. Mosquito beasties were biting my arms. Between them and this rope that did not appear strong enough to hold even my back pack, I was seriously rethinking this jungle idea. Slowly, I began to ascend. The rope was, in reality, stronger than I originally thought. Near the top, Sahaj reached through the opening and lifted me up the remainder of the way.

He circled his arms around me, "Bagheera, *really*?"

I shrugged. The room was well made. It was obvious that this was a local residence not one of those cushy hotels. The wood structure was made to be an extension of the tree itself. "What is this place?"

"Hanupreesh knew an Adivasi, Khiret, who is letting us stay here in his home. He will be our liaison to the Katakuchin tribe."

Sahaj started to roll down these huge mosquito nets around the little room. Instead of beds there were two wood futon pallets on the opposite sides of the room. Coir braided rugs covered the coconut trunk floors. There was a crude shower in the corner behind a curtain. Walking over to the bathroom area, I could see the pipes that went straight out the wall of the room. From the window, moss covered piping wound down the tree into a box at the base of the trunk. It was some sort of make shift solar collector. *Ingenious!*

"Who exactly are the Katakuchin? When do we meet this Khiret?"

"This evening he will come for us and take us to the village where we will meet the elders. The elders will decide if their assistance will be given to us. If we are dealing with magic then this tribe is an expert in black magic. They are very connected to spirits and the jungle. They are intricately connected to the very earth that India is made from."

"How do you know this?"

"Years ago when my family first arrived on the shores of India, this tribe helped bring peace to my soul, unknowingly of course. I only lived among them in panther form."

We did not have long to wait. Shortly after we dined on the smoked salmon and mangoes that we had bought at the market, Khiret arrived. We descended silently and followed the barefoot Khiret through the jungle. I had absolutely no sense of direction and instinctively wanted to mark the trees to find my way back. Sahaj seemed confident, as usual, so I would just have to trust him.

That is what made India so different to me than Atlanta. Back home, I thought I had a level of control over things. I thought I took risks. I have since realized though that I have trust issues. I grew up depending on myself just as my mom had instilled in me. I used that as a barrier between me and the world. I did not accept the same level of trust I had in myself in others. Here, I knew nothing. I had no choice but to trust others. Maybe all my previous relationships failed because of this. My current line of thought and self-reflection was sure to lead me toward depression so I tried to snap out of it and stay focused.

We went through a clearing which open up into a village of sorts. Rows of straw and bamboo huts lined a cleared circle of dirt. At the back of the row of huts was a great tree that had a tree house similar to the one we stayed in. Khiret lead us to the cleared circle and motioned for us to stand near some carved wood statues. In the center was a bond fire. Oddly, it did not feel hot. Honestly, I was hotter from the sweltering heat of the night air than from the fire. Pictures flew into my head and people carrying the same bluish fire in their hands along a cave with painted walls. After snapping back, I walked over to the fire and put my hand in pulling out a little flame that danced in my hand.

I could not help but smile. When I looked up Sahaj was looking at me strangely as well as Khiret. Another man, who had to be the chief, just gazed into my eyes. He held me there transfixed for a while. I quickly blew at my little ball of fire to distinguish it. Instead of disappearing, it turned into the shape of a woman – actually the shape of me – and walked back to the bond fire. Even I was amazed at this.

The chief continued to look at me for a few more minutes but remained silent. Sahaj stepped forward and bowed slightly to the chief. He began speaking in English which I found strange as he spoke several Indian dialects fluently. Khiret translated. "I am humbled by your wisdom and will be silenced by your actions. We come seeking help to save the lives of our loved ones, to stop the destruction of this land and to free the spirit of this girl." He motioned to me. I was taken aback. Truly, Sahaj knew more than he let on.

Khiret backed away while the chief walked closer to Sahaj. He wore a white dhoti, which resembled a long skirt wrap. His face had markings on his cheek and forehead. The cheeks had lines of various widths curving up to his eyes while his forehead was a mixture of spotted shapes.

He placed his hand over Sahaj's heart. He began chanting. The chief's eyes began to become so large I thought they would pop out. Sahaj made this coughing sound a few times then spoke to the chief in his own language. Now the chief bowed in front of Sahaj. When this happened Khiret bowed as well. I did not understand what was going on.

The chief now approached me. He placed his hand over my heart. I recognized the same chant. His eyes looked to me with sadness though.

By now several villagers were mulling around the circle. The chief called to one of the village women. She went to her hut and brought out several coconut shells. Inside them were several colored paste-like paints. Picking up my arm the chief dabbed a little blue paste down the length of my arm. It disappeared as soon as it dried. He then put purple, yellow and black on my face and it disappeared too. The woman took away the bowls.

The chief spoke to Sahaj who came to stand by my side. "He wants you to walk into the fire. He says your spirit would like to talk to you."

I was not afraid of the fire. I knew it would not burn yet I still felt nervous. Unanswered questions fed my nervousness. Taking a deep breath and opening my mind, I walked into the blue flames. The fire grew and swelled to ten times it original size. I looked out just in time to see the villagers, Sahaj and the chief jump out of its way just in time.

After a moment, a blue flame version of me showed up. She then split into three different flame versions of me. They spoke in unison and sounded like echoed whispers. "We are Kaya. We are the paths you see in your mind."

"Are you from the Siren realm?"

"No, we are Kaya."

I needed to approach this differently. "Does Kaya live just in my head or someplace more solid like earth?"

"Yes."

Okay, this was really frustrating. I am in the

middle of nowhere, standing in a fire, talking to little blue figments of my imagination. One of the Kaya stepped closer. "You are special. You can see Kaya. We will guide your spirit on this journey. Kaya is choices."

"I do not understand. Are you telling me you put the pictures in my head?"

She nodded. "Kaya is choices. We have watched you from a far. You do not abuse Kaya. You do not use Kaya for greed. Your heart is pure. Kaya will share more with you."

The three fire women circled around me holding hands dancing like little sprites on a cartoon. Suddenly they stopped. Each woman turned into a different scene. The first was people hanging shackled. The second was an ocean with two suns hanging in the sky. The third was the grove of Sirens.

"We can hide your choices from others, but only for a while. When the sun sets on the third day the magic will be seen by the seers. Kaya will guide your spirit and show you many things. Love will guide your choices but will not be enough. Fear will end your life or make you stronger. Accept what can not be changed or you will lose Kaya."

With that they were gone. The flame returned to

normal size and I stepped out to an anxious Sahaj. He had a million questions in his eyes. While I was in the fire the villagers had brought out oversized mats to eat on. The sky had also turned to a luminous night-time black flanked with sparkling white diamond stars. The jungle opened up directly over the circle yielding a fantastic view above.

The chief spoke briefly to his waiting women while the villagers began dancing around the fire. Drums of all shapes beat rhythmically in cadence with their dancing feet. They chanted rough, throaty sounds accentuated by one lone flute playing methodically. I felt the spirit of these people move around embracing everyone in attendance. One by one the drumming slowed as each villager vanished into the darkness of the night until it was only me, Khiret and Sahaj left. Khiret stood noiselessly to lead us back to the tree.

Chapter 20 – I Date A Deity

Morning startled me as I did not remember going to bed. I did not even recall walking through the jungle. What I did know was that a very large cat was pinning me down to the bed with his extremely hefty paws. Trying to move him proved futile. Even in his slumber his muscles were tensed. I screamed at him to wake up. He opened one green, coppery eye and tightened his panther grip. He blew out a little sigh making his whiskers tickle the side of my face. I yelled at him some more.

This time he morphed into a man and pulled me on top of him in one switch motion. "Is this better?"

"You were crushing me. What's up with that?"

"There are things in the jungle that are not as nice as me. I needed you near me to protect you."

"Protection? I'll have to remember that line." I started to feel just how morning it was to him and moved to slide off but his arms grabbed my waist and pulled me impossibly tighter to his body. His mouth captured mine for a very soft morning kiss.

He let out a deep, heavy sigh and let me go. I stood to head towards the shower area. "Oh, Sahaj, just for future reference, when sleeping with me that is all the reason you need to stay a man." I ducked behind the curtain. I heard a little laugh mingled with the sound of the climbing rope hitting the tree.

Grateful for a little privacy, I quickly showered and changed. My stomach began to inform me that it was time to eat. Breakfast would be slim as our fruits and vegetables were running out. I had just grabbed a banana when I heard Sahaj climbing up the tree. He was carrying packages wrapped in cotton cloth tied with a rope that hung over his shoulder.

"What's this - room service?"

He unwrapped the bundles that lay on the small table that stood by the opening of the tree house. Large banana leaves were rolled and tied. These became our makeshift plates. Sahaj punched holes in coconuts for us to drink.

He laid some white and orange logs on the banana leaves. "This is putta. It is mainly rice and coconut. This is idli, a rice and banana pancake. Here is a sweet mango sauce for dipping."

"It smells wonderful. Where did it come from?"

"It was left for us by the villagers this morning."

"That was very kind of them." Sahaj just grunted. He looked uncomfortable which made me nervous in turn. "Is there something wrong with you?" I put down my putta roll and sniffed it again. "Is there something wrong with the food?"

His eyes were soft when he chuckled. "No, the food is good. It was left by the villagers as an … offering."

"Sahaj, you took food from their temple?"

"No, woman, they worship animal spirits." He just kept looking at me as if that explained it all.

Then the big picture started to click in my head. "They worship – *you*? Oh…Ohhhh!" Silently I mulled that over.

"Does that bother you?"

"That's a question you should ask yourself. I am just sitting here wondering how shattered their faith would be if they got to know you better."

"You are such a harsh woman."

"Is that why the chief bowed to you last night? Did he sense the panther somehow?"

"Yes, the Katakuchin tribe still holds to their beliefs in animal spirits. The current chief is more in tuned than my previous encounter with the tribe. Throughout their history there has always been one chief and one chief to be. As the legend goes there was a great warrior who came down from the sky and brought peace to the land. This warrior had control over the animal and he used this control to balance the human encroaching dominance. It is told that he lived for three hundred years. Before he left he split three pieces of his soul off. One piece he placed in an animal, one he placed in a local boy and the last piece he placed in a local man. So since this time every chief has had an apprentice so to speak. They are bound together by a common language. It was the language of the great warrior. The great warrior returns ever so often to protect and rebalance the human condition. Each chief has his own animal spirit that he claims. The current chief chose the panther as his animal spirit guide. Did you notice the markings on his face?"

I nodded my head. I did remember noticing the spots. "They think that you share the soul of the great warrior because the fire last night did not burn you."

"So I am to protect you."

"Until death do we part..." He kissed my hand but I sensed sadness.

"Listen, Sahaj, I have something to tell you." I grabbed both of his hands. "I need to tell you about last night but first I wanted to say that I really like you. I love seeing me in your eyes. I adore the intensity of your heart. My mind is always racing and you help quiet the chaos. I would like you to be a big part of my life."

Moving swiftly he picked me up right out of the chair and crushed me against his chest. "I love you Keridan. Thank you."

"Okay, with the brute force. You have got to let me go."

"No, I am not letting you go ever. You just told me you love me, albeit in your own special way. I am going to enjoy this moment."

I sighed while he sat back down with me on his lap. He gave me one of those take it or leave it looks.

He nuzzled my ear and trailed kisses down my throat. He breathed me in, passionately and insatiably. It was if my declaration released his lonely spirit that had been bottled up for years. My intention was just to be honest with him and myself but he took it to an entire new level. Frankly, as his lips reclaimed the lobes of my ear, I knew I did not mind. I jumped onto this runaway train with no conductor to help navigate.

After he had better control over himself, he asked about last night. "I met the Kaya last night. What is the easiest way to explain the Kaya?" I paused to think. "As much as I can understand, the Kaya are the possible outcomes of choices. Consider every action is a string and the Kaya control where that string goes. They let me glance at what could happen if they place a string here or there. Apparently, the flashes I see are glimpses of what the Kaya do."

"They showed me three images of what possibly is going to happen. Although the Kaya were cryptic, I believe they will be able to hide the mystical aura that surrounds me but only for three days starting last night."

"Khiret and the villagers will help us search. If

you are leaving a trace maybe Nefer is too. Alexo said he no longer had his Siren abilities but he is doing something to keep the Sirens from being able to use their powers. It can only be some form of magic – old magic I would wager."

"I remember first meeting Teranodor. He spoke of his thoughts being silenced and that a great machine locked his mind. I have a good feeling that we are in the right place although I have not seen anything in this jungle that could shelter a great machine."

"Unless, it was underground. You dreamed once of an underground cavern. What if some portion of that was true? We know that Sirens use telepathy to communicate. They can phase between realms and they are connected to the elements. Alexo was captured soon after he shimmered. So there is a connection between how they travel and how Nefer is capturing them."

"You are right. We can also assume that proximity has something to do with it as well. You sensed the bad guys at the hotel in Thiruvananthapuram right before Alexo arrived."

An idea was forming in my head, but my concentration was interrupted when I heard sound from below. Sahaj moved to gather our bikes. "It's time." He held up my bike. "What will it be - bike or me?"

"Definitely bike."

"One day, Keridan, you will be begging for me." He trailed the tips of his fingers slowly across my jaw.

Two could play his game. Pulling a chair over to Sahaj, I stood on it for a little more height. I gave Sahaj the kiss of a lifetime. "One day, maybe, but not today."

He clutched his heart. "You are too much for an old man." Satisfied, I threw the bike over my back and climbed down the tree bridge.

Sahaj asked the villagers to show us the caves. They had discovered a vast amount of magical energy expended over a mountain that was about a three hour hike away. Once we reached the valley at the base of the mountain it would be another one hour hike up the mountain. Ten villagers had accompanied Khiret this morning. He and the others had their faces painted with a pale white and yellow paste that contrasted beautifully with their dark complexion. Each represented a different animal, their own personal animal spirit.

The first hour or so of our journey would be on foot. I shouldered my bike and tried to keep pace with Sahaj and Khiret. Sahaj would absentmindedly move in front of me from time to time effectively blocking the low lying branches from scraping against me. Steamy mist rose from the ground as the afternoon sun burned off the early morning rainfall. I had given up trying to control my hair. The rain and humidity combined left me with no other choice but a thick French braid tied back with some coconut rope.

I was frustrated less than an hour into the journey. The constant attack from relentless mosquitoes left little red whelps on my arms and cheeks. I wanted to chuck this whole mission and go head back to the nice hotel back in Thiruvananthapuram. I felt bad for that. I knew Robert would never give up on me if I was in trouble. I did notice that the villagers started to gravitate towards me which was a sure sign my irritation was overtaking my abilities to control my Sirens call.

We stopped to rest. A wild elephant graced our presence. It stood in a small clearing off to the left of us. I was a little wary having heard stories of wild elephants tramping down anyone who got in their way. Sahaj sat next to me on the same weathered tree trunk. He had been in the jungle too long. A fine beard had started growing on his face giving him a sexy savage look. I was about to tease him when I froze.

The elephant stopped a few feet away from me. The magnificent animal stared at me with such intensity you could almost attribute a human quality to it. The only movement was the flopping back and forth of its tail and ears.

Its trunk wrapped around my mango and ate it. Emboldened, I stroked the trunk. With its eyes locked on mine, the elephant kneeled down. Shrugging to Sahaj, I walked around and climbed on. I noticed then that the elephant was a she. I was just as awed by my new found friend as everyone seemed to be. When I was situated on top I rubbed her ears. "I think I will call you Elizabeth. Do you mind?" The elephant continued to flap her ears so I took that as a confirmation that her new moniker was okay.

As I was holding on, pictures flew into my head. A great battled was being fought. I saw a mountain then thick, grayish clouds surrounded the mountain in a split second successfully cutting the mountain into two parts - base and peak.

I looked down to Sahaj. His head came to the bottom of the elephant's ear. "I do not think we will be coming back to the tree house."

"Did you see something?"

"I think we are on the cusp of a big fight."

Sahaj went off to speak to Khiret. I settled into Elizabeth and enjoyed not have to walk at least for the last hour of the trip. We had left manmade paths a long time ago. We were deep into the jungle where human footsteps rarely fell.

Elizabeth would stop and munch on some bamboo every now and then. It definitely slowed our pace but it was still better than the alternative, at least for me. Sahaj stayed in front with Khiret as Elizabeth became twitchy when he was near. I guessed she sensed the panther in him.

Glimpses of the mountain between the tree limbs above me could be made out. We were getting closer. The forest became less dense and eventually we made our way to an opening that led to the ruins of an ancient city. Overgrown vines had completely taken this city over. Elizabeth stopped and would go no further. My ride was over. Just as quickly as I was on I was off. Elizabeth turned and traipsed back into the clearing. She seemed to not want to wait around.

Sahaj was beginning to climb the steps when a line of women came out of the forest on the other side of the city. They were striking and majestic. Khiret was talking to their leader. The closer I got to them the more I realized they were huge, tall like amazons. Their skin was dark. Their eyes were small. Their braided hair was intertwined with green vines.

Intricate designs were all over their bodies with delicate swirls on their shoulders. I had seen those marks before. Red flags went off in my head. My heart began to race. I willed my feet to move, to run. I was able to scream, "Sahaj!" From about fifty yards ahead he turned around. "I had it wrong! I had it wrong!"

Chapter 21 – Sweet Torture

My feet finally received the message and I took off running in the direction of Sahaj. Alarm crossed his face. He backed up to move towards me. I said a little prayer that what I was about to do would not kill Alexo or put him in further danger. I had to believe in Kaya.

Time crawled by but I finally made it to Sahaj.

"What's wrong?"

"Choose me."

He grabbed my hand. "I don't understand, sweetheart." At that moment he let out a gut-wrenching scream and fell to the ground. It was like an invisible chain had yanked him down.

Recognition flitted over his features. He searched the line of women. His eyes fell on one who smiled back almost childlike. "Ida."

I shook him. "Choose me. Fight it. Please." Conflict began to etch lines into his face. Those beautiful eyes that could see though me began to cloud over. "Fight it. It's not love." I pressed my lips to his hoping to force him to remember the feeling that was slowly draining from his body. "I'm not going to lose you too."

By this time Khiret and the villagers were falling back sensing something was not right. The women surrounding Princess Ida were genuinely shocked by her behavior. Sahaj found enough strength to tell me, "Careful, these women are expert archers. Their skills have been handed down from generation to generation. They were the private body guard of the Raja who once lived in these ruins."

It was taking all he had not to go to her. The strain seemed to make him age a bit. "No matter what happens, I do love you." He bowed over again.

My fist clenched and anger ripped through my body. My nails had begun to rip the flesh of my palm. Stones rose from the ground and began to circle Sahaj and me. I thought to myself, "This is just great. A lovesick woman who can kill and cause destruction with mystical arrows gets reincarnated into a person who happens to be an expert archer. I am having a string a bad luck when it comes to the men in my life!" Wind rushed around me.

Princess Ida moved towards us. "My sweet prince, why do you not come to me?" She spoke English with a heavy Indian accent. "This is the beginning of our dance."

The silence was pierced by Sahaj's scream. It must be killing him. "Princess Ida, today is not the day for this." She focused on me as if she just realized I was there. She turned her bow towards me. I concentrated on the arrow and sent it into a tree. A small windstorm jutted out of our protective bubble and blasted a rock towards Princess Ida grazing her arm. That move incensed the other women in her tribe because they began to assemble for a fight. Sahaj yelled something at Khiret. Khiret fell back with the other villagers into the jungle. Sahaj morphed into a panther then rubbed up against my leg. I deflected arrows right and left. They never relented. My mind ripped vines from the stone ruins and began tying up women one by one. I needed some help. The vines were only buying me a little time.

The ground began to shake. Elizabeth and a few of her friends barreled from behind me knocking down small unsuspecting trees in their way. She slowed slightly as she approached. I used the floating rocks as steps and leapt into the air hoping to land on her back. Sahaj ran in the middle of the pack while I called for all those deflected arrows to fly ahead of us towards the last few remaining archers. We were able to clear the ruins but without Khiret I had no idea where the cave was.

The elephants continued charging up the narrow path towards the top of the mountain. How was I to slow down this wild animal? Sahaj was running ahead of the pack now. I hoped Khiret mentioned to him the cave's whereabouts. After about thirty minutes of nonstop running, Elizabeth and Sahaj slowed. I listened and watched the trees but saw no sign of Princess Ida and the archers still in pursuit.

I slid off the side of Elizabeth and thanked her for saving my life. Who knew if she understood me or not but it seemed the right thing to do. I saw an outcropping of unusual stones off to my left protruding from the ground. It had carvings similar to the petro glyphs we were searching for. There was a small crevice on the side of the rocks. It was only about three feet wide. It looked more like an animal den than anything else. I started to crawl in but Sahaj hissed from behind me. He nudged me out the way with his shoulder and went inside. After a few moments he poked his head out and motioned for me to follow him. All my years of watching *Lassie* on television was finally paying off, I was starting to understand animal language.

Before I was too far in, I concentrated on as many small boulders that lay around the opening. One by one, I mentally stacked them to seal the opening to the cave. I did not think to find a flashlight before doing that so it took me a minute to find my back pack and the flash light in the dark.

The small, cramped corridor widened into a much larger space the further we crawled. When it was large enough to finally stand up, Sahaj morphed back into a man and both he and I collapsed down to the floor.

He pulled me over to him and cradled me in his arms. "You are my protector. The old chief had it right. How can I ever repay you for saving me?" His voice was gruff but there was a hint of discomfort to the timber.

My adrenalin was completely gone now. My anger had abated. The tears began to flow anew down my face in a continuous salty stream. I reached for some wipes out of my bag to clean my bloodstained face. "This is too much. I can't lose you. Why did Ida have to show up now? The fates surely must have it out for me. It's not like I do not have enough people chasing me down already. Are you still… in pain?"

I could not see his face clearly but his shoulder sagged a little more than they had. "Not as much as before. The cycle has started again so I will be more attuned to it. The pain…", he choked a little, "was unexpected. I have never allowed myself to be so connected to one person before. Every fiber in my being wanted to go running to Ida but my mind knew it was not right. Before when this has happened, I just gave into the feeling. It was just a part of my life. Fighting that feeling was no doubt one of the worst experiences I have ever encountered. The pain is just another nasty side effect of the curse. Now at least I know what to expect."

He was still shaking a little. "Thanks for choosing me."

"I told you that you would be begging for me someday."

I punched him. "I do not have much in me left. I am afraid that I have drained so much of Alexo's life force today that even the Kaya won't be able to hide my aura." His grip around me tightened while he place soft kisses along my hairline.

"I have a theory though."

"Enlighten me."

"Aunt Melody told me that all the missing sirens were from the air element. The Kaya showed me men shackled. I think these petro glyphs may show where they are hidden. Some type of magic is at play. That much we know, but what if Nefer is using nature to naturally enhance the power of magic?"

Sahaj shifted me a little. "I don't follow you."

"Think about the chief. He is attuned to the elements and nature…the very foundation that India sits on. He is not sitting around professing to be some witch doctor with spells to cure or curse. He is following the spirit of the animals, of the land. The Sirens are similar to the chief in that regards, at least in this world. They are a part of nature. Their abilities give them some control over the element from which they were born from."

"So you think that the missing Sirens are being held in places where air is in limited supply?"

"We are in the inside of a mountain, right now. How hard would it be to seal up a room and limit the flow?"

"So, Siren's do not need to breathe?"

He was trying intentionally to poke holes in my theory. I could tell. "Siren physiology never came up in my studies but what other conclusion can I come too?" I hoped the sarcasm in my voice was not lost to him.

He started to rub my temples. It actually did help my headache some. "Claws in. So if we subscribe to your theory, where does that leave us?"

"I don't know. I was hoping for a little of Khiret's magic to help guide the way."

"I think at this point we will have to make our own magic. How is your hand doing?"

I had not even noticed my hand scar. I briefly shine the flash light on it. "It is as small as Aunt Melody's now. Maybe if I clear my mind I will get some pictures in my head. I have never tried to get a flash. They have always just come to me."

Feeling around with my dim light I searched for a slightly larger patch of flat rock. I crossed my legs as I did in yoga class and tried to clear my mind. I slowly breathed in and out but my mind still raced in every direction. I remembered then the Kaya told me to trust my choices and to trust love. I opened my eyes and felt Sahaj watching me.

I went back over to him, sat on his lap, and began kissing him. He pushed me away. "Sweetheart, this is not a complaint, but do you think that this is the right time? What about Alexo? What are you doing?"

"I am trusting love like the Kaya said. Be quiet. I am hoping that I will get pointed in the right direction."

"Well, in that case, let me help you out." He brought me closer to him. I felt his desire grow with every kiss. His mouth captured mine and only left to place kisses on every inch of my shoulders. He then ripped my shirt and began kissing my breast. My skin burned as he trailed kisses back up my throat. He recaptured my mouth and let go of all his pent up passion. I had forgotten about Alexo, Robert and Ida until a little blue flame appeared in the room. Stunned, I pulled away. Sahaj pulled me back to him with such a force that the room echoed the thud sound our bodies made as they came back together.

"Stop!"

"What's wrong?" He was breathing heavily.

"I think it worked, look." I pointed to the little blue flame.

The light casted a surreal blue color in the corridor. He looked positively deflated. "Great!"

"Sahaj!"

He threw up his hands. "I know I went into this with the knowledge that you were just using me but you are going to have to forgive me. I can't just turn off as quickly as you can."

I could visibly see him adjusting his pants and trying to get the passion from his face. He was angry. I bent back down. "I was not using you and trust me I would love to see where this was leading but I do not think we have a lot of time." I saw the tattered remains of my shirt on the ground. "Your panther strength has annihilated my shirt. I can't exactly walk around like this." I pointed to my bra. He took his shirt off and slipped it over my head ever so slowly. The heat had not yet died out from his eyes. With his bare chest exposed, I had to catch my breath. I lightly traced the outline of his pectoral muscle and absentmindedly began to kiss his chest.

He gently pulled me away. "This is going to be difficult."

He smiled. "Well, it only seems fair that you should be in some kind of pain as well."

Chapter 22 - Ultimatums

We followed the blue flame down the corridor. I wondered where the Kaya would lead me. Would Nefer be here? Would I find the missing Sirens? I became slightly anxious even though my body was starting to feel the deprivation from being awake for almost twenty-four hours. The Kaya flame grew into the shape of a life sized version of me. She pointed to the right side of the wall then vanished.

Back in the dark, I fumbled around to find my flash light. The paltry glow was stark in comparison to the blue light that had previously filled the cavern. I felt the wall where the Kaya had pointed. My fingers felt some indentions and I threw some light that way. "Look at these. They match the ones from my dreams." I shined the light around the entire wall. "It doesn't appear to have an opening of any kind."

Something rubbed up against my leg and I screamed. I heard a coughing sound. Sahaj had morphed into his panther form and was laughing. I was about to throw my flash light at his head but thought the better of it. I still needed the light. He slowly walked up and down the stretch of wall. He disappeared completely when he went out of range of the flashlight. His fur rubbed up against me again. I still jumped a little but no screaming this time.

"The wall does not appear to be solid. The smell is different."

"I didn't think to pack an axe pick. Any suggestions on how we get in?"

Sahaj pushed all his weight into the wall. It did not budge.

"Maybe I am not meant to get in. Sirens shimmer to get around. Suffice it to say something is blocking that shimmer process. They found me when I made a connection with Alexo but it wasn't the real them." I pictured Teranodor in my head and whispered, "*Savoy Chauncii*...I can't hear you but if you can hear me I need to know if you are behind this wall."

Nothing happened and I immediately felt stupid for talking to a wall. I was not really expecting much but I had hoped just the same.

Suddenly it became hard to breathe. The air thickened and the humidity sky rocketed. "I think I set off some sort of Siren booby trap."

I was horrorstruck. "We need to get back to the entrance before it's too late."

Desperate I made one final ditch effort. I pictured the shackled men the Kaya had showed me in the fire and mentally tried to release the shackles. I waited until the pain in my chest became unbearable then I turned back towards the entrance. We made it back to the crawl space. With my last remaining energy, I blasted the rocks covering the entrance out of the way.

Cautiously I crept out of the small opening, hoping that we did not have any visitors waiting for us by the entrance. As I crossed over the threshold, the places on my skin where the chief had put the colored paste briefly fluoresced then disappeared. Outside, the fresh air soothed my aching lungs. No warrior women were in my view, but then again it was dark.

I wanted to put distance between us and the caves so we headed back down the mountain. We did veer off a little so we could take the long route around to avoid the ruins. I could not survive another run in with Princess Ida right now. Sleep and disappointment engulfed me right now.

Sahaj stayed a panther as his vision was better in the dark in that form. I held lightly to his tail as we moved through the darkness. There was a thick mist or low clouds covering the sky not allowing the moonlight to make it to the ground. He suddenly stopped and began pushing me back. My back was up against a tree and he crouched low in front of me as if about to spring on someone. Nervously, I looked around into the darkness.

Blinding, flashing, white light sparkled like diamonds reflecting the sun in front of us. Pockets of white smoke appeared depositing Sirens out of thin air one by one. There must have been at least thirty gathered around me. A smile lit my face as I recognized Teranodor walking towards me. The strain from their captivity was visible all over their bodies. Unhealed scars punctuated their beautiful faces.

"I do not know how you have accomplished it but you have freed us. We are forever in your debt." He bowed slightly but his eyes were anxious. He looked around nervously.

Some of the stress and tiredness melted away from my body. "I am glad that we found you. It is amazing how much you resemble the image from the beach." I had already scanned the crowd and the one Siren I was desperately looking to find was not among them. Sahaj had jumped into the tree behind me and was resting on a limb pretending to be a sleeping cat I presumed. "Is this everyone?"

"We need to get back home while we can. This mountain is not safe. You should head back to Sirendll as soon as possible." He thought I was Siren like he was.

The others began to shimmer away. I reached out for Teranodor. "Please before you go…I need to know was Alexo there with you? Do you know who did this to you?"

He quickly looked around him. "I am not exactly sure who all was behind it but I can tell you there are more Sirens out there in trouble. I was the first imprisoned here. I was tracking a rogue Siren when I was led to this mountain. I heard a cry for help and I materialized into a cave in the mountain. Once there I could not get out. I was linked into this machine that drained my life force. One by one more came. We could not even speak to each to other. In fact the only time we spoke to each other was when we were with you." He paused briefly, very agitated now. "Alexo was not among us. We must hurry now!"

Teranodor head shook and his eyes flashed a pale, light blue. It was so quick I thought I imagined it. Only three Sirens remained. Teranodor seemed to relax and was definitely a lot less jumpy. "You really should have left for Sirendll."

"I am not going to Sirendll. I am going to find Alexo."

He smiled slightly. "Then we are at your service." His eyes began to flash again and the other two Sirens walked awkwardly over towards us.

"I am honored but you have been trapped for some time. I know there must be somewhere else you want to be."

Teranodor leaned himself against a rock, all his anxiety gone. "I finally get to meet the beautiful Keridan in person." He smiled at me as if he told a joke and had not made it to the punch line.

"Keridan, who has been our lone piece of happiness for the past few months, there is no place else we would rather be. Besides, I am a gentleman. I would not dream of leaving you in the jungle alone at night."

Something seemed off. It just did not feel right. This did not sound like the Teranodor I had known. "Oh, I am not alone. My pet panther is with me." I hope Sahaj would take the hint play along. He jumped down from the tree behind me at the right moment. He wrapped his massive body around me. "We are just on our way back down to the village." Sahaj arched his back like an oversize kitten stretching waking up from a nap.

"No, I don't think you are."

A chill went through me. He looked at Sahaj who took a defensive posture in front of my body then let out a deep throaty sound baring all of his lethal teeth.

"Who are you? Somehow I don't think you are the Teranodor I know."

A small smirk happened across his features. "Not quite." The other two Sirens seem to be transfixed by something on the not-quite-Teranodor's back. They did not move unless he did.

I could only assume that the others were being controlled by him somehow.

He walked a little closer to me but clearly avoiding Sahaj. "You have given me some grief, Keridan." He said my name slow, punctuating each syllable. "It took me a while to find just the right body who had escaped." He touched his face. "Not too bad a choice. What do you think?"

He waved his hands and the other Sirens sat down in unison. "You see, I was made powerless but now I have all the power I could ever dream of." He waved his hand again this time towards Sahaj. Nothing happened. Sahaj was not immune to Alexo's mind tricks but some how he was not affected by this Siren. He continued. "Interesting."

My uncontrollable temper began to simmer just beneath my skin burning off any initial fear I was beginning to harbor. He finally tore his eyes away from Sahaj and focused them on me. "You are intriguing, Keridan. I think we will get along nicely."

My fatigue was gone as the surge of adrenaline rushed through my body. "Oh, I wouldn't say that. You are so absolutely not my type." As he reached out to touch my face Sahaj lunged at him. He just disappeared and reappeared playing an unfair game of cat and mouse. Shadows from the lone torch being held by one of the controlled Sirens coupled with the snarls coming from Sahaj created a menacing atmosphere. Sahaj's black fur blended with the night.

I momentarily froze as the Siren posing as Teranodor grabbed me from behind as he reappeared. My mind raced as I was trying to think of how to get out of his grasps. My Siren abilities would not work on him. Sahaj was closing in now. He whispered softly, tauntingly in my ear. "Keridan, this has been fun, but my time is almost up. I can tell you where Alexo is…I could even tell you where the human is." He paused to rake his hands roughly across my face. "But, you have to give something to get something. I'll be in touch." He let me go as Sahaj rushed him. Nefer released his control over Teranodor and his body fell to the ground. Sahaj morphed into a man and swirled me away from the body. The other two Sirens seemed to awaken from their manipulated stupor. Sahaj continued to stand in front of me while they approached. With their hands held up, they spoke slowly. "Hello, I am Jaru. This is Maris. Thank you for saving us." They moved toward Teranodor's body. Sahaj relaxed a little. "He's gone, Keridan. He can't stay in one body for too long."

I cautiously walked over to the limp body lying on the ground. His hair was growing whiter by the minute. Their voices broke me out of my shock. I lightly touched his forehead. "He does not have much life force left. We need to get him back to Sirendll."

"Do you know how he is doing this? Or how he is capturing Sirens?"

Their eyes now flashed white. I did not dream the blue before. "I could not tell you how. I was still myself when he was controlling me just unable to act independently. What he did to Teranodor was different. Nefer's mind inhabited Teranodor's body. It drains the bearer's life force much more quickly. My brother and I are lucky. He never leaves witnesses. There is a barrier over this mountain. You punctured a whole in it. Even now I can feel it being repaired."

I had an inspiration. I reached for my backpack, not knowing if I was going to ever get another opportunity. I pulled out one of the petro glyph rocks I took from Aunt Melody. "Do you know what this means?" I handed it to Maris.

He fingered it slowly. "It is part of the key. He uses ancient, forgotten magic. These marks were part of the locks that bound us. We must hurry. The repair is almost done."

"Thank you. Would you take his body to Eiliel, please?"

"We will."

They shimmered away leaving us alone again in the darkness.

After several long moments, Sahaj spoke. "We need to keep moving. Let's get off this mountain." He must have known that I needed him more as a man than a panther. He picked me up and carried me slowly down the mountain.

The trip down was much quicker than the ascent had been. I was too tired to fathom how he knew Khiret and some of the villagers were waiting for us on the outskirts of the ruins. We turned to go in the opposite direction avoiding the ruins completely. The nocturnal animals of the jungle were making sounds that grew louder the sleepier I became. Soon the forest path gave way to a true road. In the dim dawn light I could see a car with Hanupreesh standing beside it.

My sense of time was off. I did not know how long it took us to get to the car. Sahaj was thanking Khiret for his guidance while he gently placed me in the car. I was not surprised to see Aunt Melody already there. She held me tightly. Sahaj squeezed his lanky, beautiful frame in the car.

Before I drifted off to sleep, I heard Sahaj tell Hanupreesh to go to Kanyakumari.

Chapter 23 – Hallucinations And Epiphanies

I woke in a soft bed, disoriented and unaware of my surroundings. Light streamed in through the windows. I was sticky and my muscles were sore. The past couple of days came trickling back to me slowly. Just then my favorite big, black panther popped his head onto the foot of the bed and let out an over exaggerated cat stretch.

"Morning or is it afternoon already?"

Sahaj morphed into a man. "It's early afternoon actually sleepy head."

"Why did you let me sleep so long? We are losing time."

"Well, for one, you needed the rest. And,

secondly, you needed the rest."

"I am rested now, to be sure." I swung my legs over the edge of the bed. "Let me shower and change then we can make our next move." As I headed to the shower to scrub the past few days in the jungle off me, I pondered what today would bring. I needed to determine the best plan that would allow for Alexo, Robert and I to be free. I had about eight more hours under the Kaya's protection. Time was truly against me.

Nefer knew about me. How much was yet to be discovered.

I hated this overwhelming sense of failure that loomed over my head. I missed being only responsible for one person – me. How am I to fight someone who had the ability to control so much around him.

Armed with a nice hot shower, I went off in search of my family. It did not feel odd to consider Sahaj as a part of my family now. Each passing day over here seemed to stretch on for months. The few weeks I had known him must equal thirty in cat years. Was there such a thing?

Aunt Melody hummed a soft tune as I walked into the common area of the suite. I peeked out the curtain hoping to get a good view of the city but no such luck. The clouds outside matched the foreboding darkness that slowly climbed up my spine. Room service had brought up some breakfast. I knew I needed to eat but I could only nibble on some fruit. My nerves were shot.

"I spoke with Eiliel."

"How is Teranodor?"

"Not good. His life force is so depleted that I am not sure he will recover."

I grabbed her hand and fingered the faint scar on her hand. "I am so sorry."

"Thanks. Some of the returned sirens remember bits and pieces but I doubt it will be enough useful information before…" Her face colored slightly.

"Before I have to face Nefer and he drains my life force while simultaneously killing Alexo and Robert."

"Yes, before that becomes a possibility."

I shuddered a little. It was one thing for me to believe my demise a more realistic possibility than a successful mission but to hear it from my Aunt's mouth was about to be my undoing. "I am all about lists. Let's start with what we know. Nefer drains other Sirens life force in order to gain their powers. He can also inhabit a Siren but not every Siren. He mentioned finding the right body."

"The Sirens from last night mentioned the petro glyphs were keys of some sort. We know he knows where Robert and Alexo are located. And since I am still able to manipulate things we know Alexo is still alive. What we don't know is why Kanyakumari is where the show down takes place or where in the city it will take place."

Sahaj added, "We also do not know where the other Sirens are."

Sahaj's cell phone rang. He spoke quickly and snapped the case shut. "Khiret is here. That was Hanupreesh. He wanted to let me know Khiret was on his way up."

A soft knock sounded against the hotel door. Khiret walked in quietly. He wore a white cotton kurta and matching pajama pants. The long shirt engulfed his small frame. He nodded to Sahaj and approached me.

Khiret turned to Sahaj. He made some guttural noises which Sahaj seemed to understand. "Keridan, Khiret has a message for you. I will translate."

Khiret turned back to face me. His voice and Sahaj blended into one sound. "The chief has asked me to speak to you. He sends this message. *Great warrior, you come once again in a timely fashion and grace us with the wisdom beyond our forefathers. As we have been instructed by you since the Great War, we have kept the Vessel of Thoughts awaiting your return. It is not our place to know what it contains but it is our duty to help you bring back balance."*

Khiret then reached in his pocket and opened a pouch. He handed it to me and motioned for me to smell. Although I normally would go around sniffing unknown things, this I did without thought this time.

I was immediately transported to a mountain top. Khiret stood with me. He grabbed my hand and walked me to opening of a cave. We continued to walk deeper into the cave. Strangely though, it was never dark. Sunlight filtered in even in the deepest places of the cavern. We stopped by a flat bolder that was waist high. Khiret reached into his pocket and pulled out another pouch. This time it was full of stones. Each stone had a carved marking on it. He just stood there waiting for me to do something. Without Sahaj translating it was hard to figure out what Khiret was trying to tell me.

I picked up the stones one by one. Without any idea of what I was doing, I began to put the stones together in a pattern. It was like playing dominoes. When I was done, the stones glowed yellow. The markings disappeared from the stones and flew onto the cave wall in front of me.

They became pictures and words. It was like my subconscious was watching a silent film subtitled in a language that only it could understand. I could make out the world before it was the world we knew today. I saw the mountains being formed and valleys being filled with water to become the great seas.

The images changed into a grid overlaid on a map of the world. I held up my hand toward the wall and the map image became embedded in my arm. The movie must have been over because no more images flashed across the rocks. The small stones from the table had markings on them again. I walked over to the wall and placed both of my hands on it. My body was functioning without any assistance from my mind.

Two small rocks jutted out of the mountainous wall between my palms. On one rock I placed the pouch with the powder Khiret had originally given me and the other I placed a single strand of hair from my head. The rock with the hair instantly fell to the cavern floor and exploded into dust.

My body turned to leave the cave. My mind screamed at myself for understanding but was not satisfied. The mountain top began to fade from existence and the hotel room became back in focus.

Aunt Melody hovered over me with concern in her eyes. Khiret gazed at me, knowingly. He spoke again to Sahaj and then left just as abruptly as he arrived. "How long was I away for?"

"You never left this room little one. You simply made a face and stumbled back a bit. I think what ever you smelt made you a little light headed."

"To say the least..."

Chapter 24 – Missing Pieces

I felt strange sitting. It was like my body had been inhabited by another being. Parts of my subconscious began to unlock hidden portions of my mind. I was not just Keridan but Keridan-Warrior.

Sahaj grabbed for my hand to help ease my jitters but his touch burned my skin and I pulled away. A voice that sounded like mine spoke, "Keridan is not herself. Your touch hurts her."

I thought his shock must have mirrored my own. I was having an out of body experience. "What is the date?"

No one answered. I turned to Aunt Melody. "*Cailasophai,* what is the century? Can you tell me that child?"

She stammered. "I have not been called *Cailasophai* in a few hundred years and a child for longer still." Her back seem to bristle a bit. "It is the fifty-second century of the New Realm. What have you done with my niece?"

"Melody, what is this about? What has Khiret done?" Sahaj was not anxious but more resigned.

"Keridan is here. She is me. She is here to protect him, but I am here to help bring back balance. There has been great abuse. I will help but I will fade soon. Keridan is strong and wants her body back."

I lifted my arm and a lighted map of the world swirled around my skin until India was on top. "Bring me a map." Sahaj went to get a map and brought it to the table. He was careful not to touch me. On the map I began to draw lines covering the area. I put landmarks down to use as a scale measure. Even as an artist, I was amazed at the detail the map showed. I personally was not the best sketcher so this was another reminder that I was not alone in my skin.

"Energy is all around us. Life generates and renews the earth's natural flow of energy but there is a balance that needs to be respected. Something has put this world in danger. To find the problem follow this map. Remember, that even the dead gives back energy. I will return when it is time."

I felt an actual loss when I was back to myself. I was no longer whole. I looked to Aunt Melody who cried silently. "Who or what was that?"

"That was…another being. Let's just say that. There are different dimensions and realms that exist. Many of the stories that you hear about from ancient times were about other beings. He is an ancient one. The Katakuchin tribe called him the Great Warrior. When this world was young and shortly after the rebirth cycle began other beings began to cross over. He is one of the first. The Sirens found this realm a few thousand years later."

"But why are you crying. Is he a bad guy?" Instantly, I began checking myself for signs of damage.

"Bad is relative. There are different realms and dimensions that all coexist in this plane. Sirendll, for example, is a symbiotic dimension to the world as you know it. We are not however the only symbiotic existence. The warrior is from a different dimension. His world is tied to the nature of this earth. You may have heard of Mother Nature or Gaia. That is an old spirit from his dimension."

"His dimension is much older than ours. He is one of the ancients. They cared less about the inhabitants here living in your world. He has bonded with you to host his soul. In order to do so, though, he must take a piece of your soul. I cannot tell you which piece he took and you will not be able to remember what is missing. It is rape of the worst kind."

She was angry even more so than me. "Well, at this point, I don't have any energy to waste on what I have lost. I will need to table that until we find Alexo and I know where he is."

Sahaj and Aunt Melody looked astonished. "Did the warrior tell you something?"

I grabbed Sahaj's hand. It no longer burned and he seemed to relax a bit. "Not exactly him but more so the History Channel." They both laughed. "Look at the map he drew. These are eerily similar to ley lines. You know the mystical lines that show high concentrations of energy and magnetism."

Sahaj pulled me close. "We really need to get you out of the house more."

I ignored him. "Listen; here is the mountain

where the Sirens were being held." I traced my finger down a line that led all the way to Kanyakumari. "If I were to hazard a guess, any stone structure that falls on this line would be fair game for a hiding place or energy source. We know Nefer is using some ancient magic. Even the warrior said that the dead gives back energy. Think of how much energy must be in all these natural stone monuments. Thousands of year's worth of plants and animals compacting to create the stone."

"That would narrow down the possibilities."

"True, if we can find the Sirens before Nefer finds me we can at least weaken him to the point where the council can come in." I checked the clock. "We have about four more hours roughly under the Kaya's protection. After that I suspect Nefer will be able to readily find me. I just wish I knew what he wanted ultimately. Right now I am going into this blind and hoping to do more good than harm."

Aunt Melody rubbed her fingers into the small of my back melting my worries away. "I believe the warrior may have helped us." Sahaj moved slightly to reach some papers out of my bag. "Remember the legend I told you about the chief, the chief-in-training and the protector. He fought the great battle to keep the humans in check. He has come back to do the same thing. That is our missing connection."

"I am not following."

"Keridan, what if the humans from long ago wrote it down?"

I had my "aha" moment. I became so excited I kissed Sahaj to the point of forgetting myself. I began to pack up quickly. "You are a genius. We have to hurry. I know where the Sirens are located."

Chapter 25 – Bumps And Bruises

Hanupreesh tore through the streets of Kanyakumari, heading northeast out of the city. Clouds still covered the sun but the lateness of the day had already begun to take its toll on the brightness of the light. The road narrowed and small hut homes came in and out of view. Coconut trees adorned the surroundings.

After about six kilometers we arrived at Vattakottai, a granite fort built in the early seventeen hundreds. The fort entrance was a bland stone entranceway covered in moss with the word "Vattakottai" carved into a place stone above the heavy iron gates. The site fell under the domain of the Indian archaeological department but was still open for tourist.

The tour guide busied himself with a small group that was ahead of us so we slipped off to the left. We climbed the steps that led to the arch in the front wall. "This is where Dr. Kanari's body was found," Aunt Melody explained.

"Yes, I think we will find some petro glyphs here. Although this site dates back to the seventeen hundreds the stones are a lot older."

"We need to spread out and look for any glyph symbols on the wall. It will probably be small like the ones on the mountain were. Try not to look conspicuous. There use to be an underground tunnel that ran from here to the Padmanabhapuram Palace. It is said to have caved in, however that would make a great place for hiding Sirens."

We all ambled around and tried to look touristy. Aunt Melody got my attention and I made my way over. There was a small hidden glyph on the side of the wall. I put my hand on it and my mind began to detach from itself. I could feel the warrior returning.

He chanted to the rocks. Although, no words were spoken, I could hear him loud in my head. I began to sink in the ground. Shocked, I grabbed for

Aunt Melody and Sahaj. All three of us were deposited into a cavern beneath the surface. Thankfully no one was around when we dropped.

I could not see around me and the hole where we dropped from conveniently closed back up. I placed my hands on the walls and the warrior inside of me began his chanting again. Lighted glyphs lit the walls by my hands and then zipped down the corridor. The pictures were moving as if we were watching some primitive movie.

Just as quickly as he came, the warrior in my mind stilled. "I don't think I am ever going to get use to sharing my head with someone." Sahaj wrapped his arms around me. "Somehow I don't think this is the fabled underground passage that ran under the fort. It looks much older."

Sahaj morphed into his panther form and began walking ahead of us. The cavern was in actuality an underground city. The honey comb troves of rooms were hewn from solid rock. What could only be ventilation shafts jutted up to the surface. I saw no evidence that any person ever lived here. There were no pottery shards, no visible bones, no anything. In fact, if someone did live here it was as if they just vanished into thin air.

When we were in the caves before, the Kaya showed us the way. Somehow, I did not think it was appropriate to have a make-out session right now with a witness even one as laid back as Aunt Melody. We continued in silence following the lighted pictures on the wall. I stopped to watch the scene unfold in front of me. A man stood on a mountain. Chariots in the sky circled the mountain while the man raised his hands and split the mountain in half. Part of the mountain fell into the sea. The man called on the water spirits to help him fight the sky chariots. A battle ensued and the man was victorious.

Sahaj stopped about twenty feet ahead of me. "Keridan, there is a new seal on this part of the wall."

I put my hands on the wall. The Kaya told me they would guide my spirit and love would guide my choices. I cleared my mind. I small blue flame appeared in front of me and bathed me in a soft glow. This must have been the right spot so I pictured shackles like before and opened them in my mind.

The small blue flame exploded in the cavern with such a force that it sent me flying across the room slamming my head and back against the rock wall. Pictures flew into my head – a great storm over the ocean. The beaches around Kanyakumari were quickly becoming flooded. My eyes closed but my hand went to the tender spot on my head and felt the wet moisture seeping from my skull.

Sahaj was at my side immediately. He was shaking me but I could not speak. The Kaya were floating around the ceiling. They were screaming about a hole but no one seemed to notice them but me.

The glyphs stopped moving on the walls and the light began to dim. Aunt Melody became frantic. She was speaking so fast I could no longer understand her. Sahaj had ripped off his shirt, tore it the pieces and tied it around my head. Even through the enormous pain, I could appreciate the beauty his well cut chest. I tried to get up but it felt like my ribs were cracked.

One by one Sirens filled the cavern but only briefly. None lingered around to talk. It seemed like at least for all my pain some good did come out. About a hundred Sirens escaped before my world went black.

When I became conscious again, I was in Sahaj's arm. We still were in the cavern but not the same spot. The only light came from the blinding flash of Aunt Melody's eyes. There was a hum in the background, like rushing water. The first thing I saw was Sahaj. The pained expressionless look on his face made me realize that I was not right.

"Careful, love, don't move to fast." He gently kissed my forehead but held me so tightly it was a wonder I was able to move at all. "Thanks for coming back to me."

"Did I win?"

"Pardon?"

"I feel like I have been in a fight with a semi truck."

"Funny, but no. You have lost a lot of blood though. You have a nasty gash above your ear."

"How long was I out for?

"Three hours…It seemed like forever though."

"What! Our time is out. How could this happen?" I looked around anxiously half expecting Nefer to show up right now.

"There was some sort of trap. It went off when you freed them. The good news is that the Sirens have made it safely back to Sirendll."

"You say that as if there is bad news…aside from me being mangled, of course."

"The bad news is the blast closed in part of the

tunnel." Sahaj has carried you this far but unless you have some warrior tricks up your sleeve we are stuck."

Now that I was conscious I felt the burn in my chest. It hurt to even attempt to breathe and the makeshift tourniquet did nothing to lessen the pain. "The others were able to shimmer without a problem. Did you want to try?"

"No, little one, I'm not leaving you. I am also not giving Nefer any more ammunition to leverage against you."

"Well, let's find out if the warrior can be summoned. Sahaj, can you let me down?" He helped me stand. I leaned against the wall putting my hands on the cool stone. I cleared my head which was hard since I was in so much pain. I began to think about the warrior and hoped he would show up. After a few moments, the glyphs on the wall slowly began to light up. The wall beneath my hands slowly began to dissolve.

Stumbling back, I watched the opening in the wall become larger. A narrow passageway began to emerge. It was steep. Like sixty degrees steep. With glyphs lighting the way, we cautiously climbed up.

The lighted scenes began to flicker after about

thirty minutes into our ascent. I clutched the wall and grabbed for Aunt Melody. Even as Aunt Melody caught me, I screamed in pain. Her touch hurt as well. "This host is not well. I cannot stay in this body. Do not touch her!"

Panting, I steadied myself against the wall. "What do you expect us to do if we can't touch her?" Sahaj had snapped. There was a feral slant to his eyes. It gave me pause. I had to remember that it was directed towards the warrior and not me.

"This host must make it out before she dies."

Sahaj's beautiful light brown skin turned a ghastly shade of green. Aunt Melody's eyes flashed white and she began to chant fast in Sirendali.

I was lifted up off the ground and began to float up the incline. It actually hurt but not as bad as when I was touched. It felt weird. I had to shift continuously and adjust myself to stay balanced. That was definitely not enjoyable. I lost control a couple of times and was flipped upside down. Sahaj kept a healthy distance behind me looking to pounce as soon as a problem arose. He looked sick. I wanted to curl up in his arms and just rely on his closeness to salve my tired soul. However right at this moment not even love would make me endure that kind of pain willingly.

I stole a look to Aunt Melody and noticed her hair began to have white streaks in it. This was draining her life force. I wondered what the difference between her making me float was and when Alexo would fly me around to dance in the air.

Natural light filled the passageway ahead so the end was near. Rushing water sounds grew louder the further we went. We came out near a cave opening facing a body of water. I could not tell if it was the ocean or the sea. All I knew was we no longer were at Vattakottai.

Aunt Melody was spent. Her soft curls were tinged with white over half of her head. She rested on a rock at the entrance of the cave. She turned to me. "I have done my part. Now save her."

"*Cailasophai,* I understand your aversion to me. For your sacrifice, I will save the girl. There is much left to do and she will get worse before better, but you have my word."

"And her soul?"

"I exist because she exists."

I felt the warrior leave me. The pain subsided a little probably do to the extra stress he had put on me. "How much life force did that cost you?"

"Nothing to worry yourself about, little one. Right now, we need to find out where we are."

Sahaj held me as soon as he was certain the warrior was gone. The strength of his hug told volumes on the depth of his emotion. "I hurt when you hurt. This kills me to see you in pain." He kissed me softly before I realized Aunt Melody had left the cave. He was very careful not to cause my head and ribs any more damage but there was and undercurrent of pent up tension that was ready to explode.

"I wonder what our relationship will be like when there are no mythical creatures chasing us. I think after today I am so ready to go back to my normal existence." I leaned into his chest.

"It will be magically mundane." He smiled his charming smile. I wished the mundane would come quickly.

Chapter 26 – Is This The End?

"I am glad you two are enjoying the moment but we need to keep moving." Aunt Melody had appeared in the entrance of the cave.

Sahaj picked me up and we headed out towards the water. "Where are we?"

"We are at the Vivekananda Rock Memorial or at least on the island where it rests." The sunlight hung very low in the sky. The clouds were thicker than earlier and the light only hinted that a sun might exist.

Once we cleared the lip of the cave by the water, I was able to see the statue that loomed over head. I remember reading that this place was very special. It was sacred not only because the Swami Vivekananda meditated there but also it is said to have the footprint of the Goddess Devi Kumari engraved in the rock.

"Whatever is to happen will happen here. This is the place of two suns that the Kaya showed me." I looked down at myself. My appearance looked even worse than how I felt.

"You look beautiful." Sahaj rubbed my hands.

"You are biased and lie well. I will have to remember that in the future." His smile was like air...I needed it now to simply exist.

"I hear people still milling around but the place should be closing soon." I heard nothing but leave it to my Aunt's supersonic hearing to be in effect. We did however leave the cave and ventured out. I really wanted to change clothes at least. I was looking a little macabre with all this dried blood on me; but, that would have to wait until later. I did not want to draw any further attention to myself.

We went out onto the rocky outcropping that touched the water and found a little forgotten ramp. It did not look as if was used regularly and it was not man-made. Sea birds began following close. Aunt Melody's head snapped over to me.

"You must control your call, little one. I can see your aura again."

"It's a little hard to do when I can barely concentrate on anything other than my pain."

"Try harder, please. I honesty don't know how Sahaj can be so calm. Even I am starting to be affected by it."

"I think I need to find Hanupreesh, if you two ladies are going to be alright. I am sure he has made it here by now. He is ever bit as much cursed as I am. I would feel better if we had a way to get off of this rock that did not involve underground caves. We also need to get you to a doctor. You are no match for anyone in this condition – final showdown aside. My phone is dead so I will go ahead. Stay here out of the way." He kissed my forehead and I watched his lanky frame run off. He showed not much in the way of wear and tear from today's adventure.

I steadied myself against a pole that jutted out from the rock. It was a bad attempt to ensure that people stayed away from the ledge. In just our short walk we were now about thirty feet above the water. This fact coupled with my fear of heights was all my imagination needed to go into overdrive. The tree house in the jungle did not bring me the same feeling of dread. It must be just looking at the waves bashing against the rocks below.

A small group of people began a slow descent down the top of the ramp. Aunt Melody instantly moved a little closer to me but she suddenly stiffened and her eyes flashed white. She involuntarily began to lift off the ground. She was held suspended by some unseen force. Her eyes pleaded to me.

This was it. I could not see auras; but I did not need to in order to understand that what was happening to my Aunt was a unnatural thing. I could see the tops of the pointed ears and the blank expressions from the men that approached. There were five of them walking. One actually looked completely human on closer inspection.

In all honesty, being hurt helped me. I was calmer than I should have been. I made the chains from the poles grab the legs of two of the Sirens. The chains slowly snaked their way up their bodies and they dropped and rolled off the edge crashing into the turbulent wave below.

The cut on my head began to throb and leak. The others continued to walk aimlessly as if they had not a care n the world. There was not a lot of material to work with for me to slow them down. Little windstorms unfurled around my feet, picking up small pebbles and debris off the ground. My thoughts threw these rocks like bullets towards the remaining group. Three more went down.

Nefer continued to walk towards me. My strength was wavering as I began to cough up blood. I could only assume that my internal injuries were more severe than any of us realized. At the rock plateau more Sirens were coming towards me.

"You have cost me so much trouble, Keridan, but you will make a wonderful addition to my collection."

"I am not going to be a part of anything that includes you."

"Now, now, let's not be hasty." Nefer moved his hands to reveal a small wisp of smoke. The smoke grew until it was a floating stasis chamber just like the one Aunt Melody was in. This one contained Alexo. His eyes were glassed over and his tendrils were almost all silver.

Another shake of his hand revealed a wisp of smoke that grew into a stasis chamber containing Robert. He was beaten, badly and looked to be unconscious. His eyes were swollen shut and his body gaunt. The only sign of life was the labored rise and fall of his chest as he breathed.

I looked out at the sea. In the distance, ships were moving silently through the water. I was tired but my loved ones were suffering. The world would suffer more if Nefer was not stopped. No one else would be used by this man. No one else would be subjected to his sadistic lust for greed and power. Not on my watch.

"I believe you have a choice to make. I would rather do this the easy way. I can promise you will be treasured…if you live through it."

I smiled sweetly at him…at least as much as my face would allow. He wanted my powers. There was no guarantee that he would let my family go. The Kaya said I would have to live with the consequences.

"You are correct. This should be done the easy way. I do have some choices to make. Some decisions in life are transient while others are just plain wrong. Your decision to mess with my family falls into that category. But, most importantly, some decisions are final – etched in stone, over a thousand tons of granite to be exact." I placed my hands on the side of the rock and felt it become alive under my finger tips. Out of the corner of my eye, I saw Sahaj barreling down the ramp. Pictures flew into my head of this area before people. I saw the continents move across the tectonic plates. Waters of the oceans rise and fall. I saw the seas emerge from receding waters.

I willed for the warrior to correct what had been wronged. I gave my thoughts to the already energized rocks. The granite mountain lit up with glyphs just as it had in the caves. Nefer's eyes widened in shock momentarily but soon recovered. He quickly closed the gap between us and snatched my palm to his.

He did not understand. The power lust clouded his judgment. His touch burned as I knew it would, but I had already braced myself for it. I no longer had anything else left for him to take.

"Let them go if you want me to say the words." I said through clenched teeth. My family fell to the ground. "As you wish...*Korshet*."

Several things happened at once as soon as those words came out of my mouth. Nefer screamed as light shined out of all his orifices. As he stumbled back Alexo and Sahaj was trying to incapacitate him. The Sirens that had been under his control began to shimmer away one by one. The sky was lit with Sirens who were just waiting. They looked old not like the eternal beauties I have seen so far. They must have been the council of Sirens.

Nefer writhing in pain began to slowly disappear. It was not like he was escaping. He was fading, screaming his way to non existence. Sahaj turned to me. He and Aunt Melody approached me cautiously. My hair was still billowing around me when I raised my hand to pause them.

"*Cailasophai,* as promised...until we meet again."

As the warrior left me, the last shreds of Nefer disappeared as well. Sahaj caught me in his arms. We were locked in an embrace that held so much unspoken emotion. I was alive albeit in gut wrenching pain. Sahaj was with me. Alexo and Robert were alive. I accepted the love Sahaj so freely gave.

His kiss was a soft passionate reminder that now we could start our lives. It bathed my soul with sweet smelling rose water. His love refilled my burning lungs with a new air. The fire behind his kisses could not be quenched. I was ready to be swept away into the sunset broke ribs and all.

"Never forget I loved you."

This brought me out of my reverie. It sounded

like goodbye. His touch was definitely saying something else. I could not comprehend through the haze of relief filled passion what he could mean. There were definitely no goodbyes in the world I was living in.

Then I saw the storm clouds around me dancing nastily with the angry waves. In my beautiful confusion, I did not notice the hurricane forming. I just made out a small boat being lashed around like a buoy bobbing up and down. The boat had one passenger, one lone face that would haunt me forever – Princess Ida.

She was smiling and crying at the same time. Those eyes looked torn. I knew that look. Time began to slow as I looked back towards Sahaj. He was in pain. His eyes were locked in some internal struggle between his mind and his soul. His heart was pierced with a small golden arrow.

I had no more scream in me. How much more was I suppose to take? He held on to me for dear life and I held on to him. I was reliving the death of my mom all over again. I do not know how much time passed before Aunt Melody noticed the arrow piercing Sahaj. We all hugged and cried. She grabbed my chin.

The storm raged on and I was transfixed in Sahaj's arms. Hail and fat rain drops pelted me. Violent waves crashed against the rocky shore below. "Maybe we can save him, little one." Through the blurred tears I saw him fading. Aunt Melody gently pulled the arrow out. She then wrapped her arms around him and shimmered away.

I thought the rain would stop but it did not even let up. Maybe it was just a reflection of the storm that raged through me. I did notice that Princess Ida collapsed at the same moment Sahaj left with Aunt Melody. Even though it was beyond her control, I could not bring myself to feel sorry for her. My own hurt was too great.

My father cradled me in his arm, carrying me gently back down to the coast. A couple of Sirens carried the unconscious Robert behind us. There was a ship holding firm against the raging sea. The air around the ship was still no doubt a product of Alexo's abilities. We boarded right before the pain, grief, agony took over my body.

My journey to magic ended as it began with the loss of love. With the warrior taking a piece of my soul coupled with the death of my mom and now the loss of Sahaj, I had no pieces left. Where did fairy tales come from? All these Prince Charmings in my life and I could not get just one happy ending. How was it that I had to stretch my already shaky belief system to encompass the impossible world of multiple dimensions and telekinetic powers but the basic things to believe in like love was so unattainable?

In the back of my mind, shut up in a small corner, I held on to the belief that Sahaj would survive – that he would live to kiss me another day. It was a narrow shred of hope to cling to and if proven false my heart would die all over again.

Then there was Robert. What would he think when he ever became conscious again? His body was covered in bruises albeit not as mangled as my dreams were. He had to be tortured for days. He had looked so lifeless that I was afraid that he would never recover…that for all my efforts, I still could not save him.

What exactly had I even accomplished? Sure Nefer was out of the picture, but the price I had to personally pay for that feat was too great. Every masochistic lover would tell you that having truly loved someone was worth all the pain that love would cause. I was not in that space yet. I felt more like a pawn in a game. It was wrong to feel this way.

Alexo was at his wit's end trying to repair me and make me comfortable. I was detached. I was floating above every one unnoticed as the Kaya had been in the cave. I watched as I lay motionless in a room on this ship that was not affected by the storm outside. Two figures suddenly appeared beside me which was odd for even my day dreams. They were silent for a long time. They turned towards me and said, "You are the prophecy."

With that they knelt by my body. No one else seemed to notice them. Light came out of their hands and suffused my body with a reddish glow. My disconnected self instantly rejoined my corporeal self. Just as the two figures disappeared literally into the space between the bed and the wall in a single voice they declared, "And so it begins."

ABOUT THE AUTHOR

Michelle Peterson loves all things artistic and creative. She currently resides in Atlanta, Georgia with her husband and two children.

www.ingramcontent.com/pod-product-compliance
Lightning Source LLC
Chambersburg PA
CBHW072211170626
46813CB00003B/891

9780983045106